W9-ANQ-287

Married to the Badge

Married to the Badge

A Wife's Tale of Survival

Kimberly Carol Williams Davis

Blue Line Publishing

Married to the Badge

Published by
Blue Line Publishing
P.O. Box 2311
Atlanta, Georgia 30303-2311

Davis, Kimberly Carol Williams.
Married to the badge : a wife's tale of survival /
Kimberly Carol Williamws Davis. – 1st ed.
p. cm.
ISBN: 0-9711714-0-8

1. Police Spouses—Fiction. 2. Police—Fiction.
3. Domestic fiction. I. Title.

PS3554.A93497M37 2001 813'.6
QBI01-200872

Library of Congress Card Catalogue Number: 2001130656

Printed in the United States of America

Blue Line Publishing
Atlanta

Dedication

INFINITE GRATITUDE

Forgive me for the disappointments I may have caused thee,
Particularly not reaching scholastic heights so many do wisely,
Tears of regret sting my eyes, as many doors not opened for me,
For that I understand your strive for excellence so perfectly.

Not so vivid-when a little girl-your stern, unyielding ways,
My friends out deep into the night, while at home I feel a maze,
More babies than she can feed - behind bars he is looking to be free,
For that I understand your stern and strict upbringing so perfectly.

A "God fearing lady" you taught-the Lord is merciful and almighty,
I depend and lean on Him in life, my all in every entity,
He has blessed me with a loving mom full of style, class and sophistication,
I will never be able give enough to show my boundless appreciation.

Thank you for your ear,
Thank you for your heart,
Thank you for your soul,
Thank you for you love.

By Kimberly Carol Williams Davis
A poem dedicated to mother, **Juanita Robinson Williams**

MY LOVER, BEST FRIEND, BOYFRIEND, BROTHER

Oh, lover, best friend,
boyfriend, brother,
You have *become* my king,
The man of my dreams, you are like no other.

Though not right I might be,
You apologize initially,
Yet, not perfect you have been,
Your fight for our marriage is precedent.

Many tears have fallen,
Since our alliance's dawning,
Despite the drizzle when together,
The rainbow is brighter than ever.

Our love monument we built for so many years,
Our love free and uninhibited without past fears,
You always please me-make it better despite the temperament,
I commend you on your growth so immense,
My soldier, my love, my God-sent loving gent.

By Kimberly Carol Williams Davis
A poem dedicated to husband, **Tracy Davis**

**“If you keep your face towards the sunshine,
the shadows will fall behind you”**

Author Unknown

BOOK'S CONTENTS

Foreword

Over my career, I have observed and been involved in many incidents that have caused serious injury as well as death. Some of these incidents have caused me to receive broken bones, cuts, and abrasions. On some occasions, I have had to elude bullets fired by perpetrators who did not have my best interest in mind. Through all of this, the most difficult obstacles to overcome have been those associated with my marriage and the effects that law enforcement have had on it.

It is my opinion, this book reflects the obstacles encountered while Married to the Badge. It will let others know that they are not alone and that there is hope for them. After reading this story, spouses of the badge, male and female, should feel the sense of relief knowing that being *Married to the Badge* can be a positive and rewarding experience.

Tracy S. Davis

Preface

As said by many, over fifty percent of all marriages end in divorce. In this microwave society, divorce, considered embarrassing and complicated decades ago, has become easier to obtain than a marriage license. Everyone is in a hurry. Many people don't have time, not even to work on their marriage, which requires much time. The success of a marriage is proportionate to the amount of time each individual sacrifices to make it work.

Marriages involving police officers have an overwhelming divorce rate as pressures unfold in the personal lives of these men and women. It has become difficult to put energy let alone time into these marriages. Elements including, but not limited to the epidemic of crime, the effects on the fellowmen of unethical policemen, and the low wages received by these risk takers has made it nearly impossible for police marriages to survive.

While crime is an epidemic in this society, police officers have become the subject of many huge debates and high-profile cases. As crime continues to grow, police officers must "Hurt" or "Be Hurt" and "Kill" or "Be Killed" as the respect for humanity continues to decrease. This is one of man's most life-threatening careers in America.

Secondly, the general public does not realize this profession is no different from others in the respect that it is made up of ethical and unethical individuals. Yet, many police officers should be stripped of their human rights for the disturbing treatment that they have inflicted upon many individuals. This behavior has made it harder for those who are ethical to remain respected.

Finally, many police officers are not extolled enough for their efforts while receiving pay incommensurate to their skill as well as the deadly risks that they incur daily. This is the greatest travesty of them all.

In summary, how does a police officer balance the daily struggle of fighting in deadly streets and the stresses of his/her policing career while maintaining a peaceful, successful marriage? Though a marriage in which one or both individuals serve the law is different and much more difficult than others in many aspects…a marriage is a marriage is a marriage. They all require an abundance of love, pampering, devotion, attention, and God.

Acknowledgements

First and foremost thank you Lord, without you there is nothing! Special thanks to my editors Henri Forget and Lisa Davis; Brittain Wilder III, the author of Getting and Keeping your Mate Trained, Whipped, Faithful and on a Leash - you played a huge role in getting my book in print; Don Spears, the author of Good Pussy- thanks for your advice; Idella Parker, author of The Perfect Maid – thanks for your support; Paula Becht thanks for redesigning my cover; special thanks to my friends who kept me positive even when they weren't aware of it – Wanda, Jill, B.K., Cynt, Sonji, Janister, Marilyn H., Tawanda, Kenya, Helen; thanks to Phelps and Sands; thanks to my Father; thanks to many of my cousins, aunts, and uncles(too many to name) you are inspirational to me through your accomplishments; thanks to everyone on my husband's side of the family *who showed me much love*; Betty, I love you; thanks you Sandy for all of you advice and support; thanks to my mother's circle of Friends, you are so together and beautiful; Ruthie, Ann, Naomi, Juanita D., Brother J. you will be remembered; thanks to Mimi; Monsignor Edward Dillon and the members of M.A.P.E.S. – your support is so great – you are a wonderful organization, thanks for all you have done; Pastors Ben and Sherry Gaither, thank you for your realness and spiritual teachings; Scott Buhrmaster, my publicist, thank you for all of your efforts; Juanita Robinson Williams, my mother, I love you so much; Tracy Davis, my husband, thanks for your support in everything that I do, you are my all; and to anyone I forgot who contributed to this book, I thank you.

...Special thanks to the men and women who have ethically dedicated their lives to protect and serve our country!

Introduction

MARRIED TO THE BADGE, a story about the struggles a couple experienced during the husband's career as a police officer, is told by Candi, a fictional character. Candi allowed us to look at her marriage undergoing innumerable changes as her husband enforces the law. While she and her husband faced a number of problems preceding his career, the marriage was devastated as a result of it. Many negative elements plagued their marriage resulting in an infinite downward spiral of hopelessness.

A strong black woman raised Candi in a strict, single-parent home. In contrast, a couple who has been married for over thirty years reared Travis liberally. They met in Fort Lauderdale after both failed to graduate from college.

Despite their insecurities as well as an inability to communicate, they got married a year after dating. Months after the wedding date, they left for Georgia where the Police Department employed Travis. The police force became his "Brotherhood" and "Fraternity." Initially, it became his road to self-destruction as well. Their premarital problems turned into catalysts for several of the tragedies incurred in their marriage during his "Tour of Duty."

After he formed a close network with his fellow officers and experienced the extremities of world realities, the composition of his attitude changed. He was no longer the same person, viewing life differently than before. His work became part of his home life, as he faced difficulty separating the two. Placed into life-threatening situations constantly, his life was "on the line" daily.

Fighting perpetrators one minute and seeing a molested two-year-old victim the next was a difficult devoir for him to handle. It was impossible to turn work off when home. Despite his difficulty in separating home from work, he treasured his marriage to Candi.

Because the shield gave Travis power, he began to feel that he was above the law. Carrying the badge introduced a lot of fringe benefits that were not available to him before earning it. Because he and his friends exercised the power they had, problems persisted. One of the results of his abuse of power was incarceration. This was extremely devastating to Candi, a naïve and insecure person. It wasn't long before she went from being naïve to "Bad Girl," becoming a prisoner in one of Georgia's facilities, also. Confused about whether to leave or not, her husband was "to good to leave" and "to bad to stay." Travis believed in marriage, even if he caused a great number of their problems. Candi's childish behavior, at times, didn't make things better, either.

Infertility plagued their relationship as they unsuccessfully went through In-Vitro Fertilization. The emotional, financial, and mental stress from the procedure weakened the strands that barely held their marriage together.

Some of the difficulties that Candi and Travis experienced are common in many relationships. People just don't talk about these issues…so, sit back, read, and enjoy MARRIED TO THE BADGE as it enlightens you!

Chapter 1

Our Beginnings

We screamed, "Hell, yes!" as our tonsils were grasping for relief. My husband had just received a phone call from the city informing him of the new adventure that he was getting ready to embark upon. Their exact words were: "Mister Travis Dixon, you have been hired to serve as a police officer on the city's force." After he hung up the phone and told me the "good" news, we danced, sang, and jumped up and down for an hour.

Being a police officer wasn't his main interest as a kid. Like many other young males, he possessed resolute aspirations of becoming a professional athlete. At the age of eight, he started playing baseball on a youth league team called the Braves. It wasn't until he moved from left field to third base and catching a pop-up while getting hit in the head that he realized this talent for playing baseball. Playing in the minors or major leagues was all he dreamed of as a kid.

At the age of fifteen, Travis and his family moved from Chi-town to Fort Lauderdale. While in high school, he spent much of his free time at his aunt Jenny's house. Aunt Jenny was like one of the boys to Travis. There was no limit to the amount of beer or company he could have or bring over Aunt Jenny's. She was a police officer for a sheriff's department in South Florida. His admiration for her as a policewoman was great. On many occasions she'd comment that he fit the profile of what an officer should look and be like. She insisted that this would be a great career for him to get into.

At the end of Travis' senior year, he was awarded a baseball scholarship to attend UCLA. A few months later he went to school in California and played football as well. After a few years in college, Travis suffered a knee injury. He went back to Fort Lauderdale and worked different low-wage jobs.

My mother and father met in high school. They went to college in Ohio, started dating and later got married. I was born one semester before my mother obtained her baccalaureate in biology from Ohio Central State. After a year of marriage, they got a divorce, moved back to their hometown Fort Lauderdale and went their separate ways. I saw my father approximately once a year, which is certainly not as much as I should have, especially since "our yard touched his yard." Coincidentally, he lived directly behind us. He remarried and had other children. A local disc jockey turned promoter for a major record company, he was quite popular in Fort Lauderdale.

My mother told me that she would take me to visit his mother, but her lack of interest in spending time with me was overwhelming. My own grandmother abandoned me. Eventually my mother stopped taking me to see her. We went to the same church, also. After church services, I remembered coldness in the air, as she never parted her lips to say "Hello."

My mother made a decent salary working in a medical laboratory as a chemist and biologist. Despite my father not being there, she raised me in a strict middle-class environment. She molded me into a self-independent person and stressed the importance of education. Attending college was not a choice for me. It was a must. She'd always say, "Earn a degree, so that doors will be open for you in the future."

In the winter of 1983, I graduated from high school six months early and attended the University of Florida. I started on the right foot, but didn't stay there. I did everything my mother prohibited me to do while growing up. I even got pregnant, but aborted it due to my fear of disclosing my pregnancy to her. After deciding that college wasn't where I wanted to be, I went back home and worked at a few entry-level jobs. My mother was intensely disappointed in me due to my decision to leave school. In the spring of 1986 and after working many dead-end jobs, I attended a technical institute. There I earned an A.S. in electrical engineering and became employed as an electronic technician with a major medical firm.

A few months after I landed a job as a technician, my girlfriend Yvette and I began to party four out of the seven days of each week. We shopped, drank, hung out in clubs, fooled around in a music studio cutting rap tracks, worked out, went to jazz concerts as well as art festivals, "dogged," "got dogged," and did all kinds of things together. We hung out with professional boxers and football players as well as drug dealers. We didn't care who they were just as long as they had money. Neither one of us, at the time, was interested in being tied down to anyone maybe because subconsciously we felt that there was no one to settle down with. All the guys we ran into were no good. Hell, we figured, if you can't beat them, join them. So, we did what they did…"played the field."

Though Yvette played hard, she also worked her butt off for her family's business. They were one of the most successful black families in Fort Lauderdale. Her family owned one club and several liquor stores. She had an incredible body, as men would say "Baby Got Back."

Occasionally, I would squeeze time in for my boys, Varnell and Donte. These two were my niggas! We drank together, "Joned"(cracked jokes) on each other, and simply enjoyed each other's company. Varnell was a road manager for one of the local singing groups. Many times we went to his group's concert to show support. I was one of the fellas to them.

On Sundays, you better believe I got up in the morning and went to church. There was no question about it. I was still living with my mother and she wasn't having it any other way. At this time, she had become lax, because I was grown. Yet, she'd say, "If you can hang out during the week, then you can go to church on Sundays; No ifs, ands, or buts about it." After church I'd spend time with my mom and later with Yvette at their store.

One night, Yvette and I went to a reggae club. A wineglass filled with zinfandel was loosely gripped by my right hand, while the fingers on my left hand were snapping to the Caribbean beat. My attire consisted of a short black tight-fitting dress and black high heel shoes. My body was almost perfect. I was five-feet-seven inches tall and one hundred twenty-eight pounds, at this time. No one could tell me shit. I knew I looked good. While enjoying the vibe that night, I heard this guy's voice whispering in my ear. "Would you like to take me to dinner?"

I looked back to see who in the hell would ask me this. It was common for guys to spend money on me, not vice-versa…and if I spent money on a guy, you better believe I'd known him for quite a while and that he was worth every penny I spent. Was he out of his mind? I turned around and whom did I see?

"Hi, my name is Travis. When are you going to take me out?"

He was a medium-to-large built, light-skinned guy. Strike one! I didn't like lighter complexion men. I liked tall, dark, big and built men. They didn't necessarily have to be "drop-dead" gorgeous, but decent looking. I just want to be able to look at him when talking or listening to him. Bigger men gave me a feeling of unlimited protection and a sense of security.

I said, "Look, I am not interested. So go back where you came from."

I had seen the geek around town before. We had spoken to each other on several occasions, but I'd never paid any attention to him, because he just wasn't my type.

A week later, I was sitting at the entrance of Yvette's club helping her take the cover charge from customers. The club was packed. There were people hanging around the table where we were collecting money as well as outside the entrance. People were everywhere. There were police officers at the door and on the outside for security purposes. The music was thumping and the sights were something…all the fine men, of course. I was drinking cranberry and vodka and eating wings, while helping Yvette. Soon, who walks in the door?…the fool who had the audacity to ask me to take him out to eat.

He walked up to me and said, "So, you are Julia's daughter and you live at 3900 N.W. 8th Court."

How did he know my mom's name and address? "How do you know all of this information about me?" I asked.

"Well, one of my boys, the police officer out there, ran your tag for me. I wanted to get the 411 on ya."

We started to converse and I concluded that he was a nice guy. I thought he was somewhat of a square, though.

I asked him, "Were you okay that night you asked me to take you to dinner?"

He told me, "It was just a question aimed at getting your attention!"

Well, he didn't do a good job of getting my attention that night. We continued conversing. I actually enjoyed talking to him that night. I decided to give him my phone number, so that we could talk every now and then, but nothing more. The next day, when I got home from work, he had left five messages on my answering machine. I wasn't too happy about this. I thought to myself, *Damn, I made a mistake by giving him my phone number. He's going to be a pain in the ass, a fatal attraction or a stalker.* Yvette and my high school girlfriend, Wendi had each left one, also. Wendi wasn't my clubbin' girlfriend, but she was my longtime best girlfriend. She and I befriended each other and became very close in high school. Besides my family, she was the only one who stayed in touch with me while I was in college. If I wasn't with Yvette or my boys hangin', I was with Wendi. We'd either chill at her house or mine, watch movies, look at the stars to find the Big Dipper and Little Dipper and discuss the what-a-bouts or where-a-bouts of our high school classmates… who's screwing who, who was successful, who's on crack, etc. In high school, everyone had a classmate who got strung out on drugs. Anyway, everyone loved Wendi, the opposite of me in school. I was reserved and kept to myself. Wendi was an extremely popular, outgoing, beautiful human being. She was overweight, but never indulged in self-pity…back to the five messages. I called Travis with an attitude. He was so cunning and sweet that I ended up forgetting how upset I was with him, initially.

A week and a half went by and, as usual, I had five messages on my answering machine from Travis. I considered him a pain in the ass, a nuisance, a geek, but one of the sweetest guys I'd ever met. One day, I spoke with him and he convinced me to come by his parents' house. He, like me, lived with his parents. He was outside waiting for me as I pulled up in the driveway. Before I could get out of my car, he ran to my door and opened it for me. He was dressed in biker shorts and a nice tight-fitting shirt. Ump, Ump, Ump! He looked so good I could have just eaten him up. Then you know I had to size him up. Yes! The package between his legs looked stunning, also. We talked about our college days. He explained his two-day affair with this young lady who got pregnant. He and the young lady dated different people while she was pregnant. Months after their son's birth, they both moved back to their hometowns. She moved back to Baltimore and he went to Fort Lauderdale. Unfortunately, Travis had visitation complications with regard to seeing his son. Maybe the geographical distance between them in addition to the child's age were factors contributing to her apprehensiveness of letting the baby spend time with he and his family. Child support wasn't a factor. He paid it through a verbal agreement. Maybe she was just being malevolent. Who knows, but God?

He talked about the sports he played in college, his boys, and his past relationships with women. I just couldn't help but notice his body. I couldn't believe it, but I was actually melting. Just above my inner thighs, I was pumping and getting moist. My heart was beating faster and I felt weak. I was becoming extremely infatuated with this guy. I could not help but wonder if he noticed this or not. I had to keep my cool. I could not let him on to this.

As soon as he finished talking about his college days, he asked, "Could I please take you to dinner?"

Playing the nonchalant role, I said, "I'll think about it."

No sooner than I said that, he stood in front of me, face to face, looked into my eyes, and laid the gentlest kiss on my lips. After that kiss, we both moved our heads slowly toward each other. We opened our mouths. I placed my tongue inside of his mouth. He sucked on it, softly. We tongued for two minutes straight. He caressed me gently. His body felt so good. Next thing I knew, I had a puddle between my legs. Ya damn right I was going to dinner!

The next day, as usual, I had five messages from him. I called him back. He told me that he wanted to take me to dinner that evening. I agreed to it. When he came to pick me up he had a present for me. It was an adorable two-piece short set. He knew I loved short sets. Hell, that's all I wore. It was too hot for anything else. I introduced him to my mother. I thought to myself, he is too good to be true. After dinner, he brought me back home. We talked for a few hours in my mother's living room. Soon afterward he left. I then went into my mother's room to talk to her.

I told her, "You know, Ma, I like him, though he's just not my type."

She said, "He seems to be really nice. You should spend time with him, as he continues to treat you good, instead of hanging out all of the time."

Several weeks later, Travis and I started dating. There was one thing that I was unsure of, though. Now, don't let women fool you when they pretend to not care about the importance of sex in a relationship. At least for the most part, initially. Let's face it …if he doesn't fuck you right the first time, he ain't coming back for seconds, at least that's the way I felt.

It was a Thursday night. Travis and I had been dating for two weeks. The time that I had spent with Yvette had drastically decreased. She wasn't happy about that. She'd always call me up and insist that we both go out. I would spend a little time with her, but nothing like before. Travis was insecure about the close relationship that I had with my boys. So, I did not spend time with them at all anymore. We were sitting outside Travis's house by the pool, drinking melon balls. Will Downing was playing softly, the sky was clear and the breeze was refreshing. I had on a miniskirt set. As I looked up in the sky, I felt his lips on mine. We started to kiss. Soon I felt his hand moving slowly up my skirt. His large hand gently rubbed between my upper inner thighs. I was soon dripping with vaginal secretions. I then felt his finger move inside me. He soon removed his finger from inside of me, placed one of his arms under my legs, and the other against my back. He lifted me into the air and took me into his room. He lowered me onto his bed and lifted my skirt. I soon felt his warm mouth between my legs. We then started to make love and it was so good! The next morning, he prepared breakfast for me. It was waiting for me when I got up.

We spent every single day together while we dated, sometimes I think too much. We did everything together. Travis wanted to be with me constantly to the point that I thought he was obsessed with me. I wasn't used to spending that much time with a boyfriend. So, it was an adjustment for me, though it didn't take long for me to adjust. We were separable. We both worked the same hours. As soon as I got off from work, we were together. Hell, I really enjoyed being wanted so much. We spent so much time together that I was unable to spend time with any of my girlfriends. We soon became addicted to being with each other, not so healthy. Every night we ate dinner together. He always gave me money when I needed it. I never needed him, because he was always there. Anything that was his, he considered mine. He was my personal nurse when I would get cramps, as I had the worst case of endometriosis. Excruciating pain was a symptom of this disease.

He would rub my stomach and lie by my side. He was like no other man I had known in terms of attention, affection, and devotion. I even befriended his best friend, Ronald. Ronald was a very attractive, though promiscuous individual. If any one had a vagina, Ronald was on them like polish on a fingernail. In other words, he tried fucking every woman he met. He always got into trouble. He stayed in jail. He was usually faced with misdemeanor charges from fighting in clubs to driving without a license. Travis was actually the antidote to his wildness. Ronald was more civilized when Travis was around. If we weren't at Ronald's, we were at my house or Travis' house. Travis and I took several trips together during this time, also. If we weren't going to Chicago to visit his relatives, we were vacationing in the Islands, the Florida Keys or California to see his son. We had a ball!

We had our share of rough times, too, during this period. For example, we were at Ronald's house one-day watching television. I was ready to go home, but Travis wanted me to stay. I got upset, uttered some not-so-nice words, one thing led to another and soon we started arguing. All of a sudden, he punched a hole in the wall! Better the wall than I. Thank God I didn't have a lover who punched and/or beat on me. That's where I drew the line. The first time would be the last time. *Though, I did have a lover that pushed and grabbed me, but I did the same to him, also.* One day, he pushed me on the bed so hard that he made my lip bleed after I bit it. He thought I was seeing someone. I figured it was time to leave, but he cried, begged and pleaded that he'd never push me again. So, I stayed. On another day, I got upset because he answered me in a tone I felt was unacceptable. We exchanged a few words and I ended up landing a few scratches on his face. Afterward his face was filled with anger, yet he walked away without touching me (wanting to kill me, of course). There were times when we'd both be so upset with each other that we'd start grabbing and pushing each other with fury. Yet, we'd hold back to a point just before we caused any bodily harm to each other. It was potentially very dangerous. The altercations were symptoms of an unhealthy situation. No one ever got hurt, but the potential was there. At this point we should have gotten counseling, but we never thought about it at the time. *My advice to couples in this situation is to immediately seek help from your Higher Being or go to counseling.* If one party isn't willing to cooperate, then it's time to break-up. We were two cooperating individuals, but it would take time to control our fiery temperaments.

We were, also, two jealous people sharing our lives together. Neither of us was comfortable if the other person had a friend of the opposite sex. At this point, it was unheard of in our relationship. We continued to date though our jealousy problem and our temperaments were not improving.

"You know, Candi, I don't trust you as far as I can see you."

"Why not?"

"Because most of your friends are male and all of them can't be strictly platonic. I just find that one a little too hard to believe."

"Well you can believe it. Just because I have male friends doesn't mean that I am having sex with any of them."

"Sure, Candi…sure."

"Oh, what about all of those women that called you the first day I came over to your house?"

A few days after we agreed to start dating, Travis allowed me to answer his private phone a few times. Each one of those calls was from a woman. He would tell them not to call any longer. Because of the uncertainty of our relationship's longevity, who knows if he called them back.

"Candi, I was seeing them before I met you and you heard me tell them not to call here any longer."

"Yeah okay, ... are you sure you didn't call them after I left to let them know you were mistaken?"

"Candi,...please, you aren't making any sense."

"Oh, I'm making plenty of sense."

"Those male friends that you don't trust me with, kept me informed with the things men wanted and the games they played."

"Whatever."

"Okay Mr. Whatever."

I also didn't trust Travis because of my past experiences with men...*I brought extra baggage into our relationship.* At the end of my first year in college, I started dating a football player named Alex. Alex and I met at a fraternity party. Alex was the total package. He was 6'3 tall, had broad shoulders and skin that reminded you of brown sugar. Light brown eyes and a body so hot that anyone would be set on fire with one simple touch, he stayed physically fit by working out with the football team every day. We began to date a few months into the spring semester, spending five out of seven days together when we weren't in class. We went to Greek parties, the movies and studied together frequently.

Two months into our courtship, I decided to go home for the summer. He stayed in school for that summer. We talked with each other over the phone daily while I was away from college. I received flowers and gifts from him every other day. When the summer was over, I returned to college. The first person I was yearning to see was Alex. I began to really dig him. I went straight to Alex's dormitory room and knocked on the door. Ten seconds later he opened it. After opening the door, he stood there shirtless for eight seconds looking at me from head to toe with those sexy eyes and said, "I just need to take a good look at you. Ump, you look so good. I missed you very much"

All of a sudden he leaned down, placed his arms around my waist, picked me up and slowly started spinning me around expressing his joy due to my return.

"Oh, Alex, I missed you, too. I couldn't wait to see you," I said.

He then slowly put me down. As we continued to stand, I ran my hands across his chest. The soft skin on his chest smoothly covered the muscles protruding from his body. He soon started kissing me.

He stopped and said, "I, baby, am all yours…it's just going to be you and I against the world. You are the type of woman that I'd like to marry someday."

Just then someone started knocking on his door. He started walking towards it. I said to myself, "Shoot, I was liking this. *Being with him felt so good; if being with him was wrong, I didn't want to be right."*

When he got to the door, he opened it just enough to put his head through to see who it was. After he took a look at the person standing on the other side of the door, he whispered to the person, "Lydia, wait one second." He left her outside, put his head back inside, closed the door and told me, "Candi, I need to talk with my cousin. Just wait right there."

I sat down in a corner chair that faced the door. He went back outside. I heard low muffled sounds through the door for thirty seconds. Alex's teammate, Bob, stayed in the next dorm room. At times Alex and I would go over to Bob's room to play cards and drink. I decided that I would go down the hall, grab some chips from the vending machine and just peep in to say "Hi" to Bob because I had not seen him in awhile. I got up out of the chair, opened the door and noticed that Alex and Lydia wasn't there. I got my chips, decided to peep into Bob's room and noticed the door wasn't closed all the way. I also noticed some moaning coming from the door.

"Oh, Bob must have company."

Just as I touched Bob's door to close it and walk away, I heard the voice of a woman screaming.

"Oh, Alex!"

I said to myself, "Oh, Alex?…what in the…"

I swung the door open, stood in the doorway and saw Alex on top of Lydia. They were in their birthday suits. I simply closed the door and never said a word to Alex again.

It was March of 1990. Travis knew that I was the one for him, but deep down he felt that we needed to wait a few years before marrying one another due to the lack of stability we both had. At this time, we were both eager to move in together, so that we could have our own privacy. After we signed for our first place together in our first year of courtship, I expressed my discontent in shacking up. It didn't dawn on me until then that I would not be comfortable living with a man that I was not married to. I said to myself, "You can't move in with this man without being married to him." So, I denounced my plans of moving in together.

The second Saturday in March, Travis had a football game in the Bahamas. We flew to the Bahamas on a Friday afternoon with the other team members and a few of their significant others. After getting off the plane, I was reminded of the time my mother and I flew to the Bahamas when I was a little girl. Travis and I grabbed our bags from the baggage claim area and proceeded to one of the hotel's shuttle buses along with the other team members and significant others. The shuttle bus was built like a golf cart that was extended for thirty people. After the shuttle was full, a short dark-skinned man stepped on to the bus, sat in the driver's seat of the shuttle and drove off like a bat out of hell. As we cruised to our temporary living destination, we noticed how beautiful the weather was and how refreshing the island appeared. Travis and I held hands as we looked up at the clear, baby, blue skies that were sprinkled with pure white pillows of fluffy clouds. It wasn't long before we started driving beside the breath-taking beautiful navy-blue waters.

"Baby, this is so beautiful. Let's move here next week," I said.

"I'm in agreement. This is a beautiful sight...but you know what's even more beautiful?"

Soon Travis started inching his hands inside the pockets of his tight blue jeans and pulled out a small gray jewelry box. While a smirk sat on his face, he slowly lifted the small lid of the box, took a ring out of the groove it was sitting in, grabbed my left hand and continued.

"You are." As he spoke he placed the ring on my ring finger and said, "Will you marry me?"

I was speechless. He was such a sweetheart. This was a touching gesture. This is why I loved him. He was a sweet, special loving kind of guy.

"Yes, I will marry you. It would be an honor. I love you."

" I love you, too."

The guys won the game the following day and we partied the rest of that weekend. Travis had decided to propose to me, as we were both avid about living together. I guess he also respected my upbringing and wishes. I didn't have a problem with waiting, but knew I could not live with him if I weren't married to him. His family resented my standards and thought that my mother prohibited me from moving in with him. What in the hell was wrong with them? I was an adult and I my own decisions. I was the one who had to live with those decisions. Fortunately, my mother's parenting had a great impact on my life. At this point in my life she freely supported my decision making, as she knew I would have to enjoy or suffer the consequences of my actions.

It was May 19, two months after he proposed to me. The year was 1990. We had a chapel wedding. My mother and her best friend's wife, Tara, coordinated it. They planned it within two weeks. In attendance were approximately seventy people. At this time, I was still upset at my father, because he hardly ever came to see me. Asking him to give me away never crossed my mind. My uncle Deangelo, an airplane pilot, gave me away. He and his wife, Aunt Lillian, lived in New Jersey. My aunt Bettie from New Jersey and Travis's aunt Jill from California came. A few of my relatives who lived out of town were in attendance, also. Most of the people in attendance were friends of my mother's and Travis's parents. A few of our friends were also there. After the wedding ceremony, the reception was held in an upscale New Orleans restaurant where we dined on the patio. Travis's father played in a jazz ensemble at the restaurant on weekends. As a gift for us, the owner of the restaurant, Ralph, paid for the dining expenses and Travis's father provided the luxury of an open bar. I was touched by both gestures. The food was delicious; the atmosphere was cozy and tropical, and the reception simply eloquent.

Our first year was a living HELL/ NIGHTMARE! "House" was no longer played. This was real. He wasn't ready for this marriage and neither was I. I think we stayed together because we were both scared of seeing the other person with someone else. We started finding out each other's idiosyncrasies. Everything that one person did was unacceptable and done differently from the other person's preference...the way the bills were paid, the way the towels were folded, the way the rice was cooked, the way the house was kept, etc. You get the point? These were minor annoyances, but they were, in total, marriage shredders for many couples. We argued about every single thing. Though, whatever problems or differences we were having, Travis took care of his responsibilities such as bringing home every dime he made, as well as being there when I needed him. He was a good man, but he wasn't perfect. Human beings aren't. We always took turns with the household chores. He cleaned, cooked, and did the laundry, whenever I didn't and vice versa. We always cooperated with each other when it came to that. We just didn't communicate well. He was a good husband despite our differences. I never had to deal with alcoholism, drugs or other major issues that inevitably resulted a display of abnormal behavior.

I continued my career as an electronic technician and he worked on cars. We had the same routine, every day. We'd come home, either he or I would cook, we'd watch TV, make a little love, and go to bed.

One day, he got a call from his cousin Tarus. "Travis, the city of Chicago Police Department is hiring. Why don't you come up and apply?"

"Man, I'll think about it."

They talked for a good hour. Well this sounded pretty good to both Travis and me, especially Travis. His relatives, Aunt Julia, Aunt Jennifer, Aunt Donna, Belinda and his favorite cousin, Tarus, all lived there. These are the people he grew up around. Travis told me that one of the reasons why his immediate family moved from Chicago to Fort Lauderdale was to keep him out of the gangs. In Travis's neighborhood, you either joined a gang or died fighting them. He never wanted to move from Chicago, though. He was a Chi-town boy. Moving there sounded good to me, also. I was a spontaneous person, high on life. Hell, I loved to try new things! We needed a change in our lives anyway. Maybe I'd receive a higher salary in my field up there.

One month later, our first wedding anniversary arrived. It was May of 1991. We decided to move. Travis and I put our things in storage, packed our clothes and headed for Chi-town. Before we went to Chicago, however, we promised his aunt in Atlanta, that we would stop there on our way through. His aunt Jenny had relocated to Atlanta to work as a police officer for one of the suburban cities of Atlanta six months before we had gotten married. When we got to Atlanta, we fell in love with the area. The job market was booming. The scenery was beautiful. The real estate market was excellent. The place was a huge cultural melting pot. We were in awe of the vibrant city, although we stayed for only a few days. It didn't have the characteristics of a city such as New York, but it had a lot to offer. During our stay, Aunt Jenny treated me as if I was her own daughter. She tried convincing us to stay, but we told her of our plans to move to Chicago. So, Travis and I left to go to Chicago.

When we got to Chicago, we stayed with Tarus. He and his sister, Belinda, were like siblings to Travis. Tarus was a tall, dark guy. He was BRUTALLY honest, arrogant, and confident. He'd let you know exactly what was on his mind, whether you liked it or not. Timid people had no chance around him. Conversely, he was a very caring person who would give you the shirt off his back. He was very good to us. He had been employed as a police officer for the city of Chicago for about two years at the time. He and his sister, Belinda, treated us like royalty. Belinda was a very cute, medium-built young lady. Their mother, Aunt Julia, was one of the most loving individuals in the world. She was like my girlfriend Wendi. Everyone loved her. I adopted them as my family away from home.

Tracy applied for a position with the police department. We would look for jobs during the day, but by nightfall, we partied like it was the end of the world. I never knew what partying was until I got with them. Tarus knew everyone on the South-side of Chicago. A few of his close friends dropped by almost every night. We would play Whist, get drunk, and crack jokes on each other all night. Actually, Travis and Tarus did all the cracking. We'd even go clubbin' from time to time.

On one of the nights that we were out clubbin', Travis cussed this guy out because he got out of line with me. Tarus found out, after the incident was over. He got pissed off and cussed the guy out, also. They were both really protective of their loved ones as well as each other. Travis told me that while growing up he and Tarus would always get into fights with guys who got out of line with Belinda.

Two weeks passed. Neither one of us had a job. One day, I said to Travis, "We've been here two weeks and neither one of us has a job, yet. Yes, I'm having the time of my life, but we have got to find a job. Do you think we would have better luck in Atlanta?"

He said, "Yes, more than likely." So we headed back for Atlanta.

It was a stressful time for us, because we were still newlyweds faced with the problems we hadn't ironed out before we got married. Being jobless didn't help, either. After we got back to Atlanta, we stayed with his aunt. We often argued, verbally abused each other and, at times, wrestled with each other. It was a very bad time for us. Fortunately, three days after we got there we found jobs. While employed as a mechanic with a small company, Travis decided to apply to the police department. After I became a leasing agent, I continued hunting for a job in my field. We struggled and finally moved into our own apartment. This relieved a certain amount stress as we now had our own place.

One morning, while we were getting ready for work, the phone rang. Travis answered it, saying, "Hello…" he paused for twenty seconds and then said, "Yes, this is Travis Dixon."

Apparently the person on the other end of the phone continued, because Travis didn't say a word for two minutes.

Then I heard, "Yes, sir! Thank you, sir! I really appreciate this, sir!"

Travis placed the phone on the receiver and said, "Skooter, I have just been hired to work on the police force for the city."

"All right," I yelled!

We danced, sang, and jumped up and down. He was happy and I was happy for him. Yet, though I was happy for him, I didn't think too highly of police officers. The only police officer whom I admired was a long-time friend of my mom's named Ratrial, who worked for the local Sheriff and stopped by the house while on duty to check on us to see if things were okay. We lived in the area that he patrolled. Besides him, my opinions weren't too high for law enforcement officers. Maybe I started developing negative opinions due to the McDuffy incident, which occurred in Miami. In the McDuffy incident several police officers beat McDuffy, a motorcyclist, to death after he led them on a police chase. Miami went up in smoke and riots resulted when the policemen were acquitted. There was simply no justice in this incident. Also, there was a sense in my town that it didn't pay to be a black man…a view held by blacks and others in our society. It seemed as if police officers harassed young black men more than they harassed any other group in our town. And though many situations warranted police intervention, many times police intervention was unnecessary. I knew how much the general black male population despised law enforcement. I knew about the negative feelings that my male friends held toward the police. So I felt their pain, sympathized with them and shared their views to a certain extent. Nonetheless, there were many good police officers on the force. Because my husband was becoming one, I knew he would be a good police officer, as well. Yet, we were unaware of the turmoil that awaited us as he ventured upon his new career.

Chapter 11

Black and Blue

Running seven miles a day, learning criminal laws and procedures, traffic laws (the cornerstone of training), mastering self-defense techniques, training on the shooting range, learning the Emergency Vehicle Operation's course, and spending a lot of time in the "front, lean and rest" position was a day in and day out thing for Travis while he was in the academy. The "front lean and rest" position is being in a push-up's up-position with the arms fully extended. Instead of doing the push-ups one rests in that up-position for a period of time. Because of this rigid program, he was in the best shape that he'd ever been in. Though the instructors of the academy did a fine job teaching procedures and techniques in the classroom, these procedures and techniques were useless to the cadets and other officers when it came to policing the street. Fifty percent of training in the academy is never used in the streets. Training is in a non-volatile, clinical environment. Cadets don't have to worry about being sued. Cadets don't have to worry about getting complained about. Cadets don't have to worry about repercussions. Cadets don't have to worry about getting hurt, shot, or touched. Yet, the moment they step foot out on the **streets** all bets are off…all training taught in that clinical environment is out the window.

Travis told me that they are made to believe that the academy's "word" is the "word of God," but it took his first ass-whippin' to find out that this wasn't true.

In the shooting range, cadets are trained to shoot at distances ranging from three to twenty-five yards. On the streets the officers normally shoot at distances of two feet or less. Handcuffing techniques were taught in a structured manner in the classroom. If the same procedures were taken to the streets, half of the perpetrators initially apprehended by officers would get away. Cadets aren't taught to handcuff criminals who are resisting arrest. Many times, officers have to deplete the suspect's energy by throwing him around or punching him out to handcuff him. In the classroom, cadets are taught self-defense techniques and ways of using minimal amounts of force in apprehending suspects without causing excessive bodily damage to them or to the perpetrator. In the police academy cadets are taught to use an *escalating level of force*. If a person yells at an officer, it is acceptable for the officer to yell back. In other words, verbal resistance can be met with verbal force. The same goes for physical force. Yet, cadets are taught, "No forms of police brutality are acceptable." The academy teaches that it is a liability issue and that it is morally wrong. They further mention that they just will not tolerate it. Not all officers comply with this, however.

What does the academy teach the cadet? In the mean streets, what the academy teaches will make an officer "Black 'n Blue." Due to the criminal's non-complying actions, many officers would have to use great force to control that situation and any potential scenarios at a particular scene.

For instance:

"A police officer gets a call concerning a domestic call. As he arrives to the scene and runs to the door, screams of a woman's agony are heard. Upon entering through the front door, a policeman witnesses a man pistol-whipping a woman. He's uncontrollably frantic, after a rejection from his wife for another man. The officer tells him to drop the gun. The suspect stops beating the woman, approaches the police officer and spits in his face. With streaks of saliva on his face, the police officer puts in a help call. The suspect tries to punch the officer, but the officer ducks. The officer grabs him and they begin to rumble. The suspect, no amateur at self–defense techniques, has a black belt in karate. The officer, not as polished in self-defense techniques as the suspect, continues desperately in an attempt to apprehend him. The suspect punches the officer in the genitals with great force as they rumble. The officer becomes helpless. His help hasn't arrived yet. The suspect continues to beat the woman."

Travis concentrated on completing his homework and passing the exams. The police academy felt like high school to him. The environment was highly structured. Cadets were prohibited from walking in and out of class whenever they wanted to. Cadets could not be late. Every police academy day was an eleven hour structured environment. Physical training started at 6:20 a.m. and lasted until 8:30 a.m. After showering, cadets went to class for eight hours, not including the hour they were allotted for lunch. Classes were usually over around 5:20 p.m.

Travis's grades while in the academy were excellent. He held the second highest score in the class, although he was quite disappointed because he wasn't the valedictorian.

I was at home one day before Travis got home from the police academy. Sounds of jazz filled the air as I prepared dinner that afternoon. I sang with joy, jiggling my hips to Sade's beat…I sang "Is it a crime..da da da da um um um….Is it a crime?" Not hearing the front door open, I was startled when I heard it close. As I looked up, I saw Travis walking toward me. I ran up to him and planted a huge kiss on his cheek.

"Hey boo-boo," I said.

"Hey Skooter, what are you cooking? It smells good in here."

As I opened the lid on the pan I said, "Chicken cacciatore and we are also having a fresh garden tossed salad."

"Oh, cool."

"How was your day?"

"My day was fine, but I just can't wait until the academy is over. I feel like a twelfth grader in high school all over again preparing for my S.A.T.S. I'm just ready to get this over with and get into the streets. Candi, …I mean you have to ask for permission to do everything. Use the bathroom, make a call if it's during class-time, etc."

"You only have three more months to go," I injected trying to be encouraging.

Many of the police departments around the country only went to the academy for thirteen weeks. This department trained their cadets for twenty-six weeks.

"It's a three month period that I can't wait to see over."

Neither our relationship nor I was affected by the academy. It appeared to me that he worked a 9-5 job that required a few overtime hours every day. The academy was a breeze, for he and myself oppose to what was to come. I fixed him a drink and continued to fix dinner, while he took a shower. The balance of the evening we relaxed and enjoyed listening to music.

On the weekends, we would go to the Laundromat and wash clothes, as we didn't own a washer and dryer at the time. Afterward, we would checkout the scenery and attractions that Atlanta had to offer. We really didn't know anyone at the time. So, we continued to spend all of our time together. Travis wasn't comfortable with anyone in his class, because he didn't know them yet. I became close to a few individuals at work, but nothing to write home to Mom about.

One Friday evening, the doorbell rang. I answered it. Guess who it was? Ronald. I told him to come in. Travis and I each gave him a hug. He then sat on our sofa, got comfortable, and we talked about the time the three of us spent together in the past. He heard about the opportunity in Atlanta and how much we enjoyed it. He asked if he could stay in hopes of moving to Atlanta for good. So we accepted him into our home. Ronald's stay added a lot of pressure to Travis's job and our marriage.

Ronald started dating the daughter of a lieutenant who taught at the police academy. One day, the lieutenant's daughter and Ronald got into an argument that led into a physical altercation. Ronald left several bruises on the arms and legs of the lieutenant's daughter. She didn't press charges, but threatened to. Travis was really upset by the incident. If the lieutenant found out about the incident and found out that Ronald was a friend of his, the rapport between him and the lieutenant probably would have been destroyed. Several months after that incident, Ronald decided to go home. Things didn't work out for him in Atlanta.

As time progressed, there were only two weeks before Travis's graduation. I wanted to make his graduation day one that he'd never forget. We sent invitations to our relatives and friends. I collaborated with his aunt Jenny, to prepare a party for him on the night of his graduation. We planned and planned.

Finally, the day of his graduation arrived...October 23, 1992. Several of his family members came from out of town to see him...his immediate family, grandparents, a few aunts, my mother, and a few friends.

"...Please hold your applause as we call out the 1992 graduates of the city of Atlanta's Police Academy. ...Officer Anderson, Officer Atkins." An older, grim looking guy was gracefully calling out the names of the candidates to be sworn in as police officers. As the names were being called, the candidates walked up to the podium to receive their diplomas and shake the hands of the lieutenant calling the names, the police chief, and the city mayor. Once each candidate received his/her diploma, he'd/she'd walk down the center aisle of the room, out the left back door, inside the right back door, up the other side of the center aisle, down his/her row and then to his/her seat. The room was divided into five long sections. There were two sections on both the left and right sides, plus one center section. The packed audience was able to see all graduating candidates. There were approximately three hundred people in attendance to see twenty-five police officer candidates graduate. After calling out the names of ten candidates, the lieutenant said, "Officer Travis Dixon..."

Before we heard any other words from the lieutenant's mouth, there was a loud cheer from the back portion of the center section. There were thirty of us in this section. I guess our family and friends knew how important this moment was to my husband. The cheering lasted for about fifteen seconds. Everyone in the audience looked at our section. The cheering sounded like the Chicago Bulls fans witnessing a slam-dunk by Micheal Jordan bringing them up by two from a tied score.

"Whew Travis."

"Ooooh, Oooh."

"Way-to-go, baby!"

After the loud outburst of noise, a few chuckles could be heard from other audience members as the cheering diminished. They probably felt that we were a loud, rowdy group. There was one other outburst of noise other than the one for my husband....that for Camilia. Camilia was the only female to graduate in my husband's class. She was a tall, beautiful, fair-skinned, ex-college basketball player. She received a standing ovation, since she was the only one of three women in the academy class to actually graduate. Travis introduced me to her on one of the days I picked him up from the academy. She seemed to be really nice. When Travis spoke about the things they went through in the academy, he'd mentioned her along with the other fellows, at times. He said he really liked her as a friend. I had no problems with this. Originally, we didn't approve of friendships with the opposite sex in our relationship. Maybe we were maturing!

After the graduation, all of our family members and close friends headed back to our apartment complex and gathered in the clubhouse. Aunt Jenny, my mom and I had decorated the clubhouse with blue and white balloons, ribbons, and tablecloth. I tied blue and white ribbons around the champagne glasses and ordered a cake garnished with blue and white frosting, encompassing a badge with Travis's number in it. We enjoyed the delicious honey-baked ham, fried chicken, macaroni and cheese, black-eyed peas, collard greens with ham hocks, tossed salad, cornbread, rolls, liquor, wine and soft drinks. It was a very pleasant setting. The atmosphere enhanced by the nice smooth sounds of Will Downing, Najee and Sade playing in the background on our powerful high quality audio system. Everyone had a good time. This was one of the happiest days of Travis's life.

Chapter III

Tour of Duty

Several months after graduation, Travis experienced his tour of duty. This consisted of Foot patrol in a middle-class area, working 6:00 p.m.-2:00 a.m. I didn't really care for his hours that much, as we were used to working the same hours. Nonetheless, we worked through it. When I got home, dinner was always ready. During the day, he did all of the housework, cleaning, and cooking. I never had to do anything, but eat, relax, and workout. As I did in Fort Lauderdale, I worked out, regularly. Since we'd gotten married, I had gained a few pounds, but never allowed myself to exceed 132 pounds. My hard abdomen resembled a six-pack and my arms were firm and toned. My thighs encompassed a few dimples and weren't as toned as I would have liked them to be. I couldn't ask for more from Travis, however. He would surprise me by bringing lunch and roses to my job. He was a very romantic, loving, and caring person. Whenever we would get into a dispute, I wouldn't speak to him for days, until he apologized for arguing with me. Though I hardly gave in, he always apologized, even if I were wrong.

Pushing and shoving no longer had a place in our relationship. I stayed overnight at my girlfriend's after getting fed up with the unnecessary roughness that we were exhibiting. Travis got scared that he would lose me and we never got rough with each other from that day forward. Unfortunately, I had one complaint. Whenever we had an argument, we would call each other all kinds of names. We would always make up, but the respect that we had for each other left something to be desired. Despite our irritating idiosyncrasies and fussing with one another, we had good times as well.

Several months later, he received his first assignment in one of the worst areas of the city. His hours stayed the same. The majority of his calls involved shootings and homicide cases. "Cop haters" and "Cop killers" were common in this area. Chasing and fighting perpetrators were everyday occurrences for Travis. There were never any boring moments. On his second day at this precinct, he answered a call in which someone had gotten stabbed. Upon his arrival at the scene, Travis saw a seventeen-year-old boy lying on the ground with about twenty stab wounds all over his body. His head was engulfed in a puddle of blood. One of his eyes was missing and one of his ears was dismembered. On the left side of his head, lay the missing eyeball, but they never found his ear.

Later that night, the leaves from a willow tree rustled upon the windowpane and woke me up. I looked at the clock and noticed that it was past the time that Travis normally came home. I started pouring sweats of fear and nervousness. Usually between two-thirty and two forty-five, he was walking in the door. He'd call around nine or ten every night to say, "I love you, baby" or "I'm calling to say that you are on my mind." This night he didn't.

"Oh my God," I said to myself. "I wonder if anything has happened to him. Maybe someone beat him to a bloody pulp and left him to die; or maybe he got shot by one of the creeps in trying to arrest one of the gang members; or maybe a motorist didn't hear his sirens, or see him speed to someone's rescue at 90 miles per hour, failed to yield, and ran into him causing a major accident.

What am I going to do? I love him so much. He's been a very good husband to me."

I got out of bed and paced my bedroom floor for two and a half hours. I was hesitant about calling the precinct, because I'd rather the bad news come to me. Then, I heard the door open. I was so excited to know that he was alive, but I was pissed-off, also. He could have at least called and told me he would be late. It was five o'clock in the morning. What in the hell was wrong with him?

"Hey, baby, what are you doing up?" he said. He was so drunk that the smell of liquor on his breath made me drunk.

"Pooh, why didn't you call? I was worried about you."

"Skooter, I was drinking with the fellas and I didn't want to wake you up. We had choir practice tonight."

"What in the hell is choir practice for a police department?"

"That's when all of the guys get together, drink, bond, and talk about all the shit that's going on in the streets, department, etc."

Well, at that point, I didn't give a shit if he was going to a choir rehearsal, usher board meeting, or whatever. I was boiling. This motherfucker didn't even have the courtesy to call me and say that everything was okay. He was "getting a life" with his career, while I stayed at home wondering if he was okay at work. He started developing strong friendships with his fellow officers. He'd go out twice a month for drinks and talk on the phone more than a teenager…no problem. On the other hand, I was still living in the "Let's-be-together-24 hours-a-day/ 7-days-a-week" syndrome. I didn't realize at the time that I needed to get a life, too.

Two days later, Travis and his partner, Nathan, responded to a domestic call. Two guys weighing well over 250 lbs. were fighting. Apparently, the neighbors heard all of the commotion and called 911. As soon as Nathan and Travis got there, they noticed that the door was open. One of the guys was sitting on the floor holding his broken nose. The other guy was swinging a bat in his hands. Both of those guys looked like bodybuilders. As soon as bat swinger saw Travis and his partner approaching him, he said, "Get the hell out of my house."

While moving toward this guy, Travis and Nathan saw many small, scattered piles of cocaine lying around a table turned upside down from the rumble that took place before they arrived. There was also a base pipe lying in the corner.

The guy continued, "Look, this shit is between me and my husband."

That's right, they considered themselves a married couple.

The "husband" said, "Get the fuck out of my house, before I shove this bat up your ass." He was drugged up from the coke they had obviously done earlier. "Put the bat down," said Nathan. As soon as Nathan finished that sentence, Travis rushed the guy. They immediately started rumbling. Nathan grabbed the guy's hands and shifted them toward his back, while Travis handcuffed him. They arrested both of the guys. These types of dangerous calls were the norm for police working in that area.

During this time I started worrying about my baby while he was at work. After hearing the many exciting, dangerous, gruesome details about his job, it was only natural to worry. My heart would skip a beat when the phone rang. I would pace the floor if I thought long enough about the dangers he faced from day to day. It didn't take long for my hair to fall out. My skin even broke out because of the stress levels from worrying about him. The close relationship I had with my mom and the friendship that I developed with Lauren, kept me sane. Wendi's support also kept me sane. Yvette and I didn't talk much after Travis and I married.

I met Lauren while taking a karate class. She and I became close because we had something major in common. Both our husbands were police officers. I wasn't too interested in befriending many women, because I felt that women caused too much trouble. For a long time, she was the only female friend I had nearby. My preference was befriending males. My personal, friend's and several family member's experiences have revealed to me that *women have a higher tendency* than men to hold grudges, connive, create bickering bullshit, get involved in what he said or she said, and compete with one another in appearance due to their insecurities. Men appear to be less emotional than women are, so many times I don't have to worry about saying certain things the wrong way for fear of hurting their feelings. Besides, it's a wonderful feeling to be "one of the boys." You get to know what men are made of when you are not sexing them. Unfortunately, because of the jealous relationship that my husband and I shared.... male friends in my marriage was like water and oil...it wasn't mixing. It was a sacrifice that I didn't mind making, though. There was no doubt about my husband's love for me. What we had was very special, nonetheless, it was far from perfect.

A sixty-five-year-old lady called the "911" operator. She woke up to noises made by someone who had invaded her home. The intruder had driven to her house, broken and entered through her kitchen window located on the side proceeding to load his car with her possessions. After hearing the window breaking, she picked up her cordless phone, hid in the closet and called 911. Officer Carter was the first officer dispatched to handle the call. As soon as Officer Carter got to the scene, he pulled out his nine millimeter handgun, opened his car door, kneeled behind it, rolled down the car window, and pointed his gun at the front door using the bottom of the window frame of his patrol car as leverage. He then yelled at the top of his lungs, "This is the police. Come out with your hands up." The older lady, attired in a nightgown, ran out of the house to the police car in terror, escaping a potential hostage situation. Before Officer Carter said anything to her, the criminal's leg could be seen easing out of the side window of the house. Officer Carter ran to the window to apprehend the suspect. The criminal, noticing Officer Carter's charging toward him, slipped, got up and ran. While Officer Carter was running, he placed a **help** call for assistance in capturing this guy. Travis was the recipient of the call. Carter and the criminal ended up in a one-mile foot chase. En route to the chase, Travis radioed Officer Carter to find out their exact location. Through all of Carter's sounds of exhaustion and gasping for air, he told Travis their location. At this time Officer Carter was starting to lose sight of the criminal. Just then, Travis appeared from nowhere driving his car onto the sidewalk of a street between the foot chase of Officer Carter and the criminal. Travis jumped out of his car and started chasing the suspect. Close enough, he forcefully pushed the suspect off balance. While falling, his legs hit Travis's ankle, causing him to lose balance, also. The street of the foot chase had shoulder that that led to a steep ditch. The end of the street was intersected by another street. When the two fell, they began to slide for several seconds. They went tumbling down the sides of the hill over the edges into the steep ditch. The criminal grabbed Travis's radio receiver during the struggle. Travis told him, "Let my damn radio go." The guy wouldn't release the receiver. At this time, the police cars driving by looking for them had no visual evidence of the chase or struggle. It hadn't dawned on them to look over the edges into the ditch. Travis could not inform them of his location at this time. The criminal soon started punching Travis in the chest. Voices from his radio receiver asking him for his location pierced through the speaker. Travis then began to punch the criminal. The criminal then locked his grip on Travis's radio receiver. As they continued to struggle, Travis punched the criminal, again. The criminal continued to grip the receiver as his head poured blood. Soon the guy started throwing more punches at Travis. Finally, Travis punched the guy seven times in repeated motions on the same spot on his cranium. He finally released the receiver and stopped punching Travis. He handcuffed the criminal and took him to jail. Later on, Travis found out that the guy had a metal plate in his head from a gunshot injury months before this incident, which was a bizarre but logical explanation for the difficulty in subduing him.

It is quite common for police officers to work off-duty jobs such as security at nightclubs, directing traffic during rush hour, patrolling industrial areas after business hours…the list goes on. These are called extra jobs or EJ's . They often get paid double on extra-jobs compared to what they are paid on-duty. So, it is a great way for many officers to earn quick money. It's how Travis earned a lot of his money, because his base salary wasn't sufficient. He started working different EJ's a couple of hours a week. I kept him company at several of his EJ's . One of his EJ's in particular, I took great pleasure going to. He provided door security at a sport's bar every Friday night in the neighborhood he patrolled. I think I enjoyed it mostly because I was able to eat and drink whatever I wanted for free. This sports bar was beautifully decorated. On one side of the club, a signature-like fluorescent light displayed the word *Dug-out*. Behind the sign were booths of black leather seats with tables made of black marble. The hardwood floors were designed like a basketball court. A seventy-five inch television screen dominated the right side of the club/sports bar, while approximately twenty twenty-seven-inch televisions were mounted to the ceiling in other places. High round marble tables with black barstools were assembled in the middle of the sports bar. This upscale sports bar was located in the middle of a high-crime area. Travis's job was to cease all fights and ensure that no one entered the sports bar with any weapons. This was a place filled with a diverse group of people of high-spirited attitudes. Everyone seemed to always enjoy themselves during the times I went, except for one Friday night under a full moon. The sports bar was almost at room capacity on this night. There was standing room only. Many people were there to watch a play-off sports game on the big screen TV while others were there to hear the D.J. playing the latest hits. Someone had notified the fire marshal that the bar was in a possible fire code violation this night, so the fire marshal made a short visit to the bar. He directed Travis and the other officers to clear the aisles, so that the club wouldn't be fined. The officers began to ask those blocking the aisles to clear the path. I was sitting at the bar near the front entrance of the door facing the bartenders. All of a sudden I heard loud voices behind me, as the crowd in the bar got even louder. I turned my bar stool ninety degrees to my right to see what in "Sam Hill" was going on. As I turned my stool and looked, I saw Travis moving backwards in a lean while this six-foot-two-inch guy of medium build threw a punch. The guy's mouth was bloody. The punch landed in Travis's chest at the very top of his bulletproof vest. As Travis tried to lean forward and charge the guy, he slipped. The guy fell on top of Travis. I was terrified, nervous, shaking all over. I ran over to the altercation to aid Travis in desperation. I was hysterical. I could have gotten hurt.

My reaction to this situation is why wives and husbands are prohibited from patrolling with their spouses. Civilians are allowed to be observers with any policeman or policewoman, but not with their mate. Hysteria and desperation can get the officer hurt or killed. Though he wasn't on duty, it still wasn't wise for me to be at his E.J. On my way over to the fight, Travis removed himself from under the guy, got up and started punching him. Soon the other officer came and they locked him up. The guy initially was told to move from the aisle. He told Travis, "No, take off the badge. You wouldn't be shit without it." So, Travis pushed the guy, the guy pushed Travis back, then Travis landed a punch in his mouth…this is how it all started.

In the neighborhood that he patrolled, people had no respect for the police at all. Civilians hated and despised the police. If the officers handled many of the situations in that area calmly and rationally, there would be no control in those streets. As mentioned previously, many perpetrators fight back by punching or shooting their guns at the officers. Not all officers go through these situations, but many of them do.

About the time of this incident I felt an increasing need to have someone nearby I could share the experience of being married to a police officer. Eventually, Lauren and I started becoming closer.

As the weeks progressed, Travis started bonding with the brothers of his fraternity more and more every day. The police department is indeed a fraternity. The development of extremely close relationship with fellow officers was understandable, as their lives depended on their loyalty to each other.

Chapter IV

Choir Boys

In the fall of 1993, I landed a decent job as an electronic technician that later resulted in a technical writing position with a Fortune 500 company. Travis continued working EJ's here and there. Eventually, his hours changed to the morning watch. The hours for morning watch were 11:00 p.m.-7:00 a.m. His days off were Sundays and Mondays. I started school again, so that I could work on earning a baccalaureate degree. Though we worked different hours, we spent our evenings together, just as most couples do. He'd usually work his extra jobs on the evenings I was in school. It wasn't a bad schedule for us. He'd come home in the morning after working all night and go to sleep, while I was on my way to work. When I got home, he would get up and start dinner. If he weren't up, I'd start dinner. Sometimes we would throw some meat on the grill. Afterward, we'd either rent videos from the video store, watch movies on TV, or read a book.

On Sundays, we would go out for breakfast, lunch and dinner. On this day we would catch a good movie at the theater, go see a play or go to a concert. At this time I was obsessed with trying to get pregnant. I wanted to bear Travis's child. After going to the gynecologist's office, I found out I had major reproductive problems.

In January of 1994, my OBGYN performed surgery on me, after finding cysts on both of my ovaries, tube blockage, and an excessive amount of scar tissue and adhesions in my uterus. Travis took care of me for several weeks until I was well. He gave me bed baths, clothed me, fed me, changed my pads, and everything you can possibly think of. He was terrific. Weeks later, I was back to normal. For several months we tried to conceive a child, but still without success. Every time my menstrual period came on, I got really depressed and cried. I didn't reveal this to Travis, though. Around him, I always stayed upbeat.

By now, Lauren started experiencing problems with her husband. She and her husband had every problem that you can think of, except for domestic violence. She would call me in tears just about every week, but she hung in there for a little while. On my end, I could see the clouds of the storm, but I wasn't sure how heavy the rain and thunder would be. Mondays became the day I dreaded. After spending beautiful Sundays with my husband, Mondays were bound to be tremendous letdowns.

My husband became part of a group that was inseparable. They only spent time together on Mondays and on "choir rehearsal" days, but they paged each other and called each other constantly throughout the day. All of the guys belonging to this clique were single, except for my husband. They had also been on the force about as long as he had been. Derrick, Winston, John, Brad, Vincent, Gary, and my husband were a fraternity within the fraternity. It was impossible to get closer than they were.

When the guys went out on Mondays, they went to strip clubs and sports bars. Travis told me that going to strip clubs didn't faze him, because he was accustomed to seeing pussy on his beat all the time. Yeah, hmmm. There was a strip club on his beat to which he answered calls. Great, this really made me comfortable. I understood the camaraderie between him and his friends, as their lives depended on one another, but enough is enough. The formation of this clique got closer and closer. If anything happened to one person, the other person was there to handle the situation. If anybody looked cross-eyed at any members of this group, that person should consider him/herself dead.

One evening, Travis, Vincent, Brad, and Derrick were out cruising the streets. They stopped at a gas station. Brad and Vincent got out of the car to purchase a few snacks and pay for gas, while Travis began to pump the gas.

As they got their items and headed back to the car, they heard Travis telling this young man, "That's all right. I'm not interested in that man."

The guy, about thirty years old and dressed in a sweat suit, wanted Travis to buy three compact discs for the price of one. From a seven–foot-wide table in width on the curb near the gas pump farthest away from the attendant he was selling a variety of c.d.'s. Maybe no one had purchased any from him that day, because he was very contemptuous. After Travis' reply, he said, "Screw you, sorry son of a bitch."

Why did he say that as Brad and Vincent walked up? Vincent immediately jabbed the poor guy in the mouth, knocking him to the ground. A few of the guy's teeth fell out. Soon Brad started kicking the guy in the face. After the guy stopped moving, they jumped in the car and sped away.

Oftentimes they would act as if they were Robin Hoods. They set out on what were called "thunder-runs," catching suspected gamblers and drug dealers by surprise. If the unsuspecting perpetrators left money behind, they would call the attention of the neighborhood needy and yell, "Free money for the taking." This is how they gave back to the community.

I, on the other hand, befriended two more women. They were my coworkers Lauretta and Jennie. We took our breaks together and worked the same hours of overtime, together. At my job, one could set his or her hours and work as much as twelve hours a day, seven days a week, overtime included. The money was excellent when we worked overtime. There were times that I'd bring home twice as much as Travis made. Lauretta and Jennie shared a lot of secrets with me, but I rarely talked about any changes that were going on in my personal life, with my husband or his career at this time.

Knock, Knock, Knock. It was twelve p.m. the following Sunday, when we heard a few knocks at the door. Who could this possibly be? Travis opened the door and shouted with excitement. "What's up man?" It was Frank. Frank and Travis practically grew up together. He and his parents decided to move to Georgia from Fort Lauderdale. They'd already bought land and were having a three-hundred-thousand-dollar home built. Until the house was built, they resided in an apartment. After reminiscing for an hour, Frank left his number and went back to his parents' apartment. Frank was a real nice, twenty-five-year-old guy. His parents spoiled him rotten. He didn't have to work, so he didn't know what responsibility was. Almost every day, Frank would bring a different girl to our apartment. He'd use the extra room as if he was at a "Motel 6." One of our bathrooms separated the extra room from our bedroom. Despite the separation, the bathroom didn't muffle the noise of women's moaning, screaming, and groaning that I heard from the spare room when they were fuckin'.

After several months passed, Frank and his parents moved into the new, beautiful six-bedroom home. The place was lavishly decorated. Everything contemporary that you could imagine was in this home such as a kitchen island, intercom with a stereo sound system in every room, TVs in the wall, etc. Frank's parents were both retired. His father was an ex-New York city police officer and his mom was a retired housekeeper. They became affluent by making wise investment decisions with their earnings. His parents decided the best place to get a home and spend retirement was in Georgia. And they did just that, at least for a little while. It wasn't long before Frank started spending lots of time with Travis. He eventually started coming to our apartment almost every other day. Travis and I were hardly ever alone.

Soon he started hanging with Travis's clique on Monday's. He became an official member of this "fraternity" that Travis was a part of, because he spent a lot of time with them, was the son of a career policeman, and was a good friend of Travis's.

Chapter V

Keeping it in the Streets/Keeping Love Alive

Travis started developing a hostile attitude. His job was getting to him. If he had the slightest inclination that anyone was getting out of line with him, he would cuss one out before it was confirmed. He was never violent at home, but his patience was extremely limited. He was frequently on edge and irritable. He started experiencing difficulties separating life at home from events that occurred at work.

Even while at home, Travis pondered the terrible ghostly things that he'd seen at work. The battered two-year-old girl whose father raped her wasn't easy for him to forget, especially, as the girl's mother, whose veins were collapsed from heroin tracks, didn't care. The thought of the woman who committed suicide by running onto the highway in front of a truck also plagued him. After the truck hit her, all that could be seen were shredded pieces of meat. The only distinguishing elements of her body were a piece of leg and a portion of her head. The rest of her body was mangled beyond recognition or repair. It looked as though her body had been through a meat grinder.

Travis's life was always on the line, because of the life-threatening situations he faced daily. Fighting perpetrators one minute and being a sensitive, loving husband thirty minutes later was a difficult transition for my husband to make. THE HEAT WAS ON! He started becoming really stressed at work. In spite of this, he continued to be a good husband. There wasn't a doubt about the pressures he was faced with, but meanwhile I didn't know the extent of it.

People would ask me how I handled being married to a police officer or what was it like being married to one. I would tell them that I experienced the same changes as any other wife would in a daily marital relationship. Whether or not it was true, this is how I felt. Hell, I didn't know what other couples normally experienced. You never know what goes on behind closed doors. Nonetheless, I felt that my marriage was typical. Normally, it was equally full of ups and downs. *Yet, later, our downs were probably closer to hell than that of others.*

It was May of 1994. Two years had passed since Travis had been on the force. The day of our fourth wedding anniversary arrived. We had a beautiful day. He took a few nights off from work so that we could enjoy two full days together.

It was ten o'clock that morning when the doorbell rang. When I opened the door, I saw two-dozen red roses each in a clear cylinder-shaped vase, a box of chocolate candy, and a bottle of white zinfandel. Behind these roses was the deliveryman from a flower shop around the corner. I took the gifts, said thank you to the deliveryman, closed the door, ran to my husband with excitement, and landed twenty kisses all over his face. I knew they were from him.

"Oh, Pooh, this is so sweet."

"Happy anniversary, Scooter. You are the best wife that anyone could ask for. I love you more than anything in this world."

"Oh, baby, thank you for my anniversary presents. I have something for you."

I went outside, opened the trunk of my car, picked up this small box wrapped in wedding paper, and took it back into the house.

"Here, baby, this is for you," I said. He opened the present. "Wow, baby!" he screamed. Sparkling and glittering in the box was beautiful herringbone necklace. He started hugging me.

"Scooter," he said while hugging me and looking into my eyes, "I love you so much. I don't know what I'd do without you."

As I looked at him, I could see an extra-thin layer of fluid accumulating in his eyes as if he were starting to cry. "I know, Pooh, I know," I said.

We then both made a toast to each other and to our love with our favorite wine, zinfandel. That day we had lunch at the Underground, browsed around a mall, went to the movies, dined at a Bone's Restaurant in Buckhead, took a carriage ride after diner, went home to watch a few porn movies, and made love for several hours. Both of us had a memorable day.

Our routine continued. I'd come home around four o'clock in the afternoon, wake him up with a kiss or with a little love making; change into comfortable clothes while he started dinner; help him finish cooking and eat. We'd then watch television or read together until it was time for him to go to work. By then, it would be my bedtime. The next morning, he'd wake me when he got home, and I'd get ready for work while he got ready for bed. This was a normal routine, as were his Monday nights out with the boys. He never missed one Monday with his "frat boys" for a year unless we were out of town or if it were a holiday. For Travis, Monday's night of "four hours" with the boys eventually became, "twelve hours" with the boys. He would call me about three o'clock that day to let me know that he was headed out to the gym to play basketball with his boys for several hours. Later they'd shower, get dressed, and head out to the sport bars and strip clubs. I wouldn't see him until about three o'clock the next morning. I really didn't think much of it, at first, because this was his outlet for his job-related stress. He didn't go anywhere any other day, so this was fine with me. It was only healthy that we spent time at least once a week with our friends. The only stipulation was time. We agreed upon a time at which we both had to be home. Call it a curfew or whatever you want, but it was what we were both comfortable with. We had rules. We tried to maintain limits, at least. Unless there was an emergency, three o'clock was the time that we both had to be in the house, if we were to go out.

Chapter VI

Internal Affairs

Early one Tuesday morning about three-thirty a.m., the phone awakened me. *Wait a minute*, I thought to myself. *This nigga ain't even here.* I picked up the phone. "Hello."

"Hi, baby." It was Travis. The tone of his voice was a sorrowful whine. "Could you please come pick me up from downtown? Internal Affairs picked me up at B.B's SportsBar. I got into a fight there a few hours ago."

Now why in the world would Internal Affairs apprehend Travis, if he were just fighting? And why in the world was he fighting? Who in the hell was he fighting?

"Travis, you are what and where? This is ridiculous. So, in other words, you are in trouble."

"Just come down and pick me up, please. I'll explain everything to you when I see you."

"Well, where are you?"

"I'm on Fort Park Street and Tenth Street on the second floor of this tan building next to the McDonald's on the corner."

"Okay, I'm on my way," I said.

As I walked up the stairs to the second floor, I wondered how long it would be before the building underwent demolition. The building smelled and looked as if it were one thousand years old. I saw a door marked Internal Affairs. So, I assumed that this was where my husband was. I opened the door and saw him sitting in a chair. His shirt was partially torn and his face was filled with anger.

"What in the hell happened, Travis? I have to go to work in three hours."

"Candi, just calm down. I'll explain everything to you when we get home." Just then, this gray-haired man approached Travis, and handed him a cup and asked him to urinate in it. Travis got up and proceeded to the restroom. I guess the old guy had to make sure that the urine was Travis's. So he watched Travis, while he pissed.

Afterward, they seized his gun. OH, NO, NOT THE GUN…EVERYONE, PLEASE, A MOMENT OF SILENCE. Now, Travis never went anywhere without his gun. It didn't matter if we were headed to the corner store one-half mile from our home or on a trip 600 miles away, he was carrying that gun. He and that gun were inseparable until it was taken away from him. As we were heading home, Travis started telling me what had happened.

"I am so pissed. Man,…" he said with anger.

"It's okay, Boo. I'm all ears," I said.

"Me and the fellas were at BB's chillin' and drinking. We'd just come from the park playing basketball. Derrick, Frank, Winston and I were all at a table, when we heard two guys at the next table arguing with each other. Soon, one of the guys arguing and his friends rushed the other guy. They started kicking his ass. They soon bumped into our table and knocked over our drinks. That's when I said, 'Hey, watch out, you are knocking our shit all over the table.' One of the guys in the brawl said, `Who the fuck are you? I don't give a shit about you or your table.' I stood up. He swung at me. I ducked, stood up, punched him and the brawl began. Derrick and the rest of the guys jumped in. Soon the police came. They started trying to break it up. We disclosed who we were to one of the police officers. Then he voiced his opinion by saying that he didn't give a damn about my badge and that I was a perpetrator just like the rest of them. The officer grabbed me. I told him to get his fuckin' hands off of me and we wrestled a little. We tore each other's shirts in the process. A sergeant showed up at the scene and called Internal Affairs."

"Baby, don't worry about it. Shit happens!"

"They suspended me for three days, pending an investigation."

"What! Whatever happened to Derrick, Winston, and Frank?"

"Well, Frank was taken to the hospital to get some of his cuts treated. Derrick and Winston were told to go home. I'm the only one that got into trouble, because I got into an altercation with the ass-hole cop."

After we got home, I had only one and one half-hours before it was time for me to get ready for work. I lay down to rest. I was tired as hell, but I got up and went to work that day, anyway. At work that day, I acted as if things couldn't be better at home. In contrast, I was so damn tired that day that I could have used my purse as the pillow and the hard floor as the bed.

A few months rolled around. Travis continued to hang out with the guys on Mondays. During this time, I befriended a male classmate. We were in the same class for three consecutive semesters. In addition to being in the same class, many times we'd study in the library together an hour before class and in class. We became good friends. But I was slightly apprehensive about telling Travis this. His name was Cory and he was tall, dark, and handsome. We shared a lot of laughs with each other. He confided in me about the relationship that he was tired of being in. The young lady that he was dating didn't appeal to him any longer and he felt that they had nothing in common. I knew he was interested in me, but I was too scared to get involved with anyone. I loved my husband. At that point, I wouldn't dare think of cheating on him.

One day, Cory introduced me to his girlfriend. She attended the same school as we. I always spoke to her and remained cordial with her when I saw her. Yet, because she knew Cory really adored me as a friend, she became intimidated by me. I really didn't realize this until he broke up with her.

In the past, I had mentioned to Cory that my husband was a police officer. He knew things such as the area Travis worked in and a few of the stories that he told me, but never the details of my marriage. Apparently, while Cory dated this chick, he eased her conscience by telling her that I was married. He also told her my husband's name and the area he worked in. By telling her that I was spoken for, Cory tried convincing her that we were just friends. After their breakup, she got upset with me. When Cory broke up with the tyrant, he inadvertently made thing difficult for me. Hell, it wasn't my fault that he no longer wanted her.

It wasn't difficult for anyone to get in contact with a police officer as long as they knew the city or county he worked in. One day Cory's girlfriend decided to call Travis at work.

He hadn't gotten in yet, so she told Travis's sergeant to relay this message to him:

"Please tell your wife to leave my boyfriend alone. They are always together and its ruining our relationship. I'm sure they are fucking each other, so you need to handle this situation before I handle this myself. My name is Katie and my boyfriend's name is Cory. I know your wife's name is Candi. She attends the same college that my boyfriend and I do. Handle your business, please."

At the time Katie called the precinct, Travis was on his way to work. When Travis got to work, the sergeant pulled him aside and told him what Katie had just said. I'd just finished my one-hundredth sit-up when the phone rang.

"Hello," I said short of breath from exercising.

"Candi, what in the fuck are you up to?"

"What do you mean, Travis?"

"Who in the hell are Katie and Cory?"

"Oh, Cory is this guy that I attend class with and Katie is his ex-girlfriend."

"Well, I just got a message from my sergeant, who received a call from Katie. Katie told him to deliver me a message about you fucking with her boyfriend."

"What, she said who…look, I'm not seeing anyone's boyfriend. She's just upset that Cory and I are friends. She's also mad because Cory doesn't want her any longer."

"All I know is this shit is all over the precinct. The word is out that my wife is fucking another man. Derrick came running up to my car to tell me before the sergeant told me."

"Travis, I love you, Pooh. I wouldn't dare mess around on you."

"And you never mentioned a Cory to me."

"Well, we are just friends. I didn't mention him because I thought that you would be jealous."

"Look, we have been together for four years. It's time that both you and I start trusting each other more."

That sounded like a good plan to me.

Chapter VII

The Non-functioning Womb

It was summertime in 1994. We decided to drive to Baltimore to pick up Travis's son, Quinton, so that he could spend the summer with us. Quinton was four then. He was an adorable little boy. Lauren and I spent more time together then, as her cute little girl, Tia, was the same age as Quinton. We had a lot of fun with the kids. Aunt Jenny's kids kept Quinton on the days that Travis and I had to work or during the evenings that we went out. Travis and I enjoyed spending time with him. Having Quinton around made me more obsessed with wanting to have kids. So, Travis and I started concentrating on conception. We had sex every day for about four weeks. My cycle was like clockwork. I could just about predict the exact hour that my period would begin.

One day, my period was a day later than I had calculated. I got really excited. Travis did, too, but not as much as I did. The following day, I felt cramps. An hour later, I wiped blood from my vagina after urinating. I was so disappointed. About one week later, it was time for Quinton to spend time with Travis's parents in Florida. So, Travis met his brother at the halfway point between Atlanta and Fort Lauderdale. Quinton stayed there for several weeks, then his grandparents sent him home. At this point, Travis really wanted kids. Because Quinton's visit brought closeness to our family, he wanted me to have his child. So, I went back to the gynecologist and then Travis and I tried to conceive for a few months. Because I didn't conceive during this period, my gynecologist referred me to an In-Vitro Clinic.

A few weeks passed before we decided to check out this In-Vitro Clinic. We finally made an appointment and went in for a consultation.

"Good Morning, Mr. and Mrs. Dixon. My name is Dr. Brown." As he looked over my records from the previous gynecologist, he continued, "It looks like you have stage IV endometriosis, Mrs. Dixon. This means that you have scar tissue and adhesions all over your uterus. It also appears that you have cysts on each ovary and both of your tubes are blocked. This is what has been causing you difficulty in conceiving. Stage IV means that on a scale from I-IV, IV is the worst."

Travis and I both looked at each other with despair.

"Though, there is hope for you two in bearing children. You have to go through a process called In-Vitro Fertilization. Unless you go this route, your chances for having a baby are maybe one percent. The other methods of conception for you would be useless."

Travis said, "What does In-Vitro involve?"

"In short, we take your sperm, Travis, and mix them with Candi's eggs. Candi would have to give herself several different shots a day for about four weeks depending upon her body's reaction to the drugs, so that we can stimulate her follicles. Follicles house the eggs. Travis, you would have to give her one of her many daily shots. This shot has to be inserted just above her buttocks. We take control of your reproductive system, Candi. Let me warn you that this procedure causes a lot of stress, physically, mentally, and possibly financially for both of you. Candi, one of the shots that you will take is going to make you feel like you are going through menopause. Hot flashes are one of the side effects. Now, before proceeding with In-Vitro, we are going to have to perform surgery on you. We need to get rid of the scar tissue and adhesions as well as the cysts on your ovaries. Keep in mind that these will come back, because the only way to get rid of endometriosis is through a hysterectomy. Two weeks after your surgery we can get the process started. Any questions?"

"Gees, I just went through surgery a few months ago," I replied. Then I looked at Travis.

"Wow, Travis…what do you think?" I said feeling reluctant about this procedure.

"Baby, it's up to you. As long as you are happy, I am happy. If you don't mind going through this, then let's go for it. I really want to have kids, but sweetheart, I'll leave it up to you."

Right then and there, I told Travis and the doctor that I'd like to go through the procedure. Afterward, he sent us to the financial consultant to tell us the costs involved. Having a financial consultant ready to meet with us sounded like this shit was too expensive for us. After the consultant stated the approximated costs, we were stunned.

Travis and I both said, "Fifteen thousand dollars!" Hell, we didn't have that kind of money at that time. We were just barely making ends meet. We told her that we'd check our insurance to see if this procedure was covered. They warned us that most insurance companies didn't cover this type of procedure.

The following day, it was confirmed that my insurance covered In-Vitro fertilization, but I had to pay twenty percent of all costs until my out-of pocket expenses totaled twelve hundred dollars. Afterward, I would be covered one hundred percent. Travis' didn't cover this, but we didn't care. Because mine did, we were happy as we could be under the circumstances.

One week later, I underwent surgery. The surgery was called laporoscopy. They dissected me in four places. After surgery, Travis nursed me to health as with my previous surgery.

Two weeks after that, I started the In-Vitro procedure. For twenty-one days, I gave myself two shots a day, one in the morning and one at night. I administered these injections in my thigh. I knew how diabetics felt when they self-administered insulin shots. After the twenty-one days, I started receiving four shots a day. I gave myself two and Travis administered the other two in my buttocks. I felt like a damn pincushion. It was awful. In addition to the bruises that started surfacing all over my thighs and buttocks, I started getting hot flashes. I even noticed mood swings. So did Travis. Travis managed to handle the stress of his job while comforting me as we went through this process. I became a total bitch during this time because of the hormones that my body was producing. Emotionally, it was a rough time for us.

"Candi," Travis was yelling from the bedroom. I was in the living room when he said, "Its time for me to give you your shot."

"Okay, Travis…I'm coming."

He prepared the shot that stimulated the follicles that produce eggs. As he was mixing the diluents with the powder, I came into the room. He then said, “Which buttocks do you want to get this injection?”

“I don’t care. You choose.”

He chose the buttock, wiped me with alcohol and gave me the shot.

“Oouch!”

“You okay?”

“I’ll be fine.”

“You know what, Candi?”

“What?”

“I know we have our ups and downs, but I love you and want us to work through all of our problems. No one said marriage is going to be easy. To add icing to this cake, my job is heavy as well. Work is unbelievably stressful and sometimes it’s hard for me to shut work off.”

“I know…I know.”

“But we are going to get through whatever and we are going to make it.”

“Boo-Boo, I’m willing to work through our problems, if you are.”

“You need to start trusting and believing in me. I know you get upset when I go out on Mondays, but I have to have some type of outlet after chasing perpetrators, fighting and getting shot at all day; I have got to have some way of releasing that stress. Do you understand, Candy?"

"Yes, I understand. I know it's emotionally hard for us with the IVF, also. I'm sorry, if I seem like a bitch. I tell you what…if I get upset with you I will count to twenty, take a deep breath and tell you that I need to talk. Can you do the same with me?"

"Most definitely…I think this is a good solution."

"You listen to me without interruptions while I speak and I will do the same for you."

"It's on."

It was time to retrieve the eggs. Travis and I were both in this operating room. I was prepped, in stirrups, and anxious to see how many eggs were going to be retrieved. My doctor began to insert this probe-like device up my uterus. I felt a slight pain, but he proceeded. There was a fluorescent-lighted screen to my left and Travis was standing to my right.

Soon the doctor said, "We have one and it's good. Look at the screen."

I looked with excitement. The instrument in which all of my eggs were to be housed was attached to the screen in such a way that we could see each egg.

Travis then said, "All right, baby."

They continued the egg-retrieval process for thirty minutes. After the medical team finished, I had fifteen eggs. While I was in recovery, Travis had to go into one of the offices and ejaculate. He was not happy about this, I found out later. Earlier, before we left home that morning, I performed oral sex on him, so that we could collect his sperm. Apparently, we didn't get to the office in time to allow them to prepare it for my eggs. After the retrieval, I went home and relaxed for the rest of the day. Travis and I were very excited.

Two days passed, then we got a phone call from the office. They told us that twelve of the fifteen eggs accepted the sperm. We had twelve embryos. The doctor told me to come in the next day for an embryo transfer. I went in the office the following day. He transferred six embryos and he froze the other six.

For twelve days, Travis treated me as if I were a fragile, newborn baby. We were very excited, but nervous. I was extremely careful, though. Meanwhile Lauretta and I were becoming closer friends. Her husband reminded me a lot of Travis. She had a beautiful little girl, also. She was one of the few people who knew I was going through In-Vitro. Though a few years younger than me, she was just like a grandmother...having a remedy for everything. She would fuss if she thought I lifted a finger. She would come over, cook and/or bake cakes for me when Travis had to work. She was a very dear friend despite the differences we may have had.

I took the pregnancy test. We found out a day later that it was negative. When the nurse at the clinic told me the test results, I felt lifeless. I was drained, emotionally. My body was tired from taking six weeks of shots. I cried for hours. I could have just gone outside, stood on the main highway from our home and let a car hit me. I was devastated. Travis was very disappointed, also. We had gone through all of this for nothing. For two weeks, I was a basket case, emotionally. During the In-Vitro process, Travis didn't go out on Mondays. Once the In-Vitro was over, Travis ended that break. He was up and out every single Monday. There was really nothing that I could say, because I know he needed an outlet to relieve some of the stress that he had from his job, the In-Vitro procedure, as well as everything else. This was okay with me.

Chapter VII

Too Good to Leave/ Too Bad to Stay

It was a Monday. I'd come home from work about four o'clock…the usual time. Travis wasn't home, but he'd prepared dinner for me. So I ate. Two hours later, the phone rang. I picked it up and answered, "Hello!"

"Is Travis home?" I heard the sexy voice of a female on the end of the line.

I tried thinking nothing of it and said, "No, I'm sorry he isn't. Would you like to leave a message?"

"Hi, I'm Valencia, tell him that I apologize for not being able to see him tonight, but maybe we can get together next week."

Before I could say anything, she hung up. I was shocked. Could my baby be messing around with this chick? I believed that he was. All this time, I thought that he was only crazy about me.

Maybe he was seeing this chick every Monday. I thought he was an innocent person when it came to infidelity. I just couldn't imagine him with someone else. Besides, I thought that I was doing Travis a favor by being with him. Was I guilty of taking him for granted? Was I giving him all that I could give to make him the happiest husband on earth? As I started asking myself these questions, I noticed that I wasn't happy with my answers. Maybe, he decided to get involved with her because there was just too much stress in our household. I could understand why, if he did. But wait a minute; this was still no excuse for going out and cheating on me. Maybe, I should pack my bags and leave. But where would I go? Hell, I knew I needed to go somewhere. Even if he said he didn't screw this chick, as far as I was concerned, he should have. I wasn't going to believe anything differently.

No more than twenty minutes had passed, when Travis drove up. He walked in the door and said, "Hey, Skooter."

"Who the fuck is Valencia?" I said with anger.

"I think I know who this person is. I arrested her boyfriend and she begged me not to take him to jail. I told her to get out of my face. Then she said she'd find out whatever she could about me, so that she could screw me over. I'm not sure if this is the chick, but I would be surprised if it wasn't."

I never had physical evidence of their being together. But, I knew how devious women were. I also knew that my husband was under a lot of pressure at home and work.

"I'm getting out of this house and I want a divorce." I shouted these words as I started packing my bags.

"Baby, I swear I never cheated on you. Yes, I know what it sounds like, but believe me."

As I finished packing an overnight bag I said, "Get the hell out of my way. Explain that shit to Valencia. You don't have to explain to me anymore, 'cause I don't want ya."

I swung the strap of the bag on my shoulder and started walking toward the door. He stood in front of the door and blocked it so that I couldn't get through it. I tried using my body weight to push him out of the way. Yeah, right, this was going to get him out of my way. He picked me up, took me into the room, and placed me on the bed face down. He then used his body weight to pin me, so that I couldn't get up.

"Candi, I swear to you that I didn't mess with that girl," he insisted.

The following night, I didn't come home after work. I tried figuring out the validity of this situation. He was good to me, but I wasn't staying in a relationship with someone who cheated on me. I spent the night at Lauretta's house. I didn't even want to see him. Three minutes after seven o'clock he started paging me. He continued doing this every hour on the hour until five o'clock the next morning. This was the second time that I'd ever stayed out the entire night.

The following morning at work, before I even walked in my office, I could hear my phone ringing. It stopped when I entered my office. Before I could get my purse into my storage cabinet, the phone started ringing again. I wasn't sure about Travis's faithfulness any longer. I was really hurt. It didn't matter if he'd slept with her, I would always have in the back of my mind the thought of him fucking another woman. That didn't take away from how good a husband he'd been, but I really didn't know what to believe or think. Obviously, he had some type of dealings with her. To what extent, I was unsure. Then I became curious to know what he would say. So, I picked up the phone.

"Bi-Optics Division, Candi Dixon speak..."

Before I could even finish, he cut me off. "Hello, Mrs. Dixon, where have you been? I've been worried, sick about you." I heard a few sniffles between some of his words. "I don't want to lose you. You are my world. I can't function without you."

"Anyway, Travis, don't call me that name anymore. I'm not interested in you and I definitely want a divorce."

I really didn't want a divorce. I just wanted clarity to this situation. I wanted to know if he was unfaithful to me. And if it were true, WHY? I knew it would be difficult for anyone to replace him, despite his temper. He was one of the most attentive husbands a wife could have. At least, I thought this was true. My friends' husbands didn't pamper them as he did me. Who else would be a househusband for or nurture me back to health or apologize to me, even if I were wrong? I know that I was a difficult person and that not too many people would put up with me.

"What time are you coming home? Please, stop this. Candi, please."

"Travis, I'm coming home, but to pick all of my things up."

"Let's talk about this when you get home."

"We'll see… whenever I come home…If I come home."

I put the phone on the receiver and continued my day, I acted as if I were the happiest person on earth. Feelings of misery ran through my body. I started envisioning my husband making love to this woman. As butterflies fluttered inside my body, my heart pounded faster and faster. It was almost impossible for me to hold back my tears. My heavy workload helped me through that day. Staying busy kept me from being hysterical.

Later that day, I went home a little earlier than normal. On this day, I raced to get home. I really didn't want to admit it, but the thought of my husband sleeping with someone else or that another woman was interested in him made me more sexually attracted to him. That didn't erase the pain that scared me. When I walked through the door, I acted as if I really didn't care about him any longer. He was already awake and washed up. His look was melancholy.

He held out his hands and then said, "Come here, so that I can hold you." I walked over to him. He wrapped his arms around me and said, "I love you so much. I'm not going to let you go."

Just then there was a knock at the door. It was Winston, one of his closest friends/Frat members and fellow officers of the police department/fraternity. Travis opened the door.

Winston came inside frantic and out of breath.

"Man, an hour ago, someone ran into Gary's car head on. Gary's airbag saved him, but he has suffered second-degree burns all over his face. He's in the hospital, now."

"That's messed up! Get the fuck out of here! Are you serious?" Travis said in disbelief.

"Man, he's at the Forsyth General.," Winston said as he tried convincing Travis.

Travis turned to me. "Baby, grab your things. Let's go to the hospital, right now. Where are the keys?

"There, over on the coffee table, ...I'm ready," I said in a hurried fashion.

At that second, I had forgotten about our problems. I was concerned about Gary as well as the effect this would have on Travis. Winston, Travis and I went to the hospital. We found out that Gary's burns were bad, but the doctor said with ointment and cocoa butter he would recover. Gary stayed in the hospital for two days. He then went home.

Over the next week, I was haunted by thoughts of whether Travis was unfaithful. Hell, if he hadn't known her, my constant nagging him about whether he did or not, probably drove him to know her. I couldn't get that ordeal out of my mind for weeks. The though of it drove me crazy.

I called my mother the weekend that followed the incident. Our "mother-and-daughter" relationship had evolved into a close friendship. She had treated me more like a responsible adult, after I got married and moved away. It was Friday night following the incident that took place on Monday. Travis had gone to work. There was no answer at my mom's place, although it was eleven o'clock. She was usually home by this time. I called again, three hours later. Still, there was no answer. I waited until six o'clock the next morning. She never picked up the phone. Where could she be? My cousin Maxine would know, because they usually told each other their where-a-bouts and what-a-bouts.

I called her up. "Maxine, do you know where my mommy is?"

"Yes, Candi. She went to a jazz concert in Vero Beach with her girlfriend Katie."

"When is she coming back?"

"Well, not until tomorrow."

Hell, I couldn't wait until tomorrow. I needed to talk to my mom today. I was desperate. I felt like a full pot of rice boiling on the stove, getting ready to spill over. I couldn't hold it in. The next best person to tell this to was Maxine. She was like a second mom to me. When younger, I would spend every other weekend with her, her husband, and their five kids. They were my extended family. All of her kids were older than I, yet we were close. I always looked forward to going over to their house when I was a young girl. At this time, she and her husband were separated. I loved him to death, because he was like the father I never had. They had been married for over eighteen years.

"Maxine, do you have a minute?"

"Yes, Candi. What is it?"

"I think Travis is messing around on me. Some chick called and gave me the impression that she and Travis are involved with each other."

"Candi, your husband seems like he is a good person. You need to pray about it, put your trust in God, and try to gain some trust in Travis. Now, you know that women are ferocious at times. So, try to believe what he's saying."

My family, Maxine and her kids, Cousin Annabelle and her family, as well as my mom, all loved Travis. They thought he was the sweetest person. He always made everyone laugh. So maybe Maxine was just being partial to Travis. Plus, you know in the older generations, people stayed in their marriages until death. The husband could have been "dog of all dogs," but the wife would still hang in there.

"Maxine, do you really think that Travis cheated on me?"

"Honestly, Candi, No!"

She didn't mind telling the truth. "Thanks, Maxine. Please don't mention a word of this to your children or anyone else."

"Oh, Candi, I won't. You don't even have to say that."

"I love you."

"I love you, too." We both hung up.

The following day, I called my mother constantly. No one could make me feel consoled the way my mother did. Talking to her and getting her advice would bring closure to the way that I was feeling. I finally got in contact with her.

She basically said the same thing that Maxine said and more. "...Candi, I understand how you are feeling. But you don't need to worry about that. I really don't think that anything happened between Travis and the girl, if he knows her. You do, however, need to start treating your husband as well as he treats you. If you don't treat him right, baby, someone else will. And he is a good man." She did have a point.

I decided not to leave Travis, but I didn't speak to him for days. My poor friend Lauren told me several days after my shocking phone call that her husband had gotten someone pregnant. I felt bad for her. I could partially relate to her, but then again we were talking about the pregnancy of her husband's lover. Lauren was faithful and committed to her husband throughout their marriage. I wondered, why would he want to cheat? Was he tired of the monotony surrounding their relationship? Nonetheless, her problems were serious compared to mine. I consoled her during this time and tried to be there for her at all times. She was definitely a better person than I. After all that, she and her husband were still trying to work through this tragedy together, at least for a little while. She even got pregnant during their reconciliation period.

Travis started taking me to Lugan's every now and then, on Mondays. The bartenders treated him as if he were one of the owners. They knew which drinks were his favorites. They knew the other guys in the "fraternity" just as well. I had an enjoyable experience the first time I went. They knew I was in school, where I worked, and my occupation, etc. They even mentioned how much Travis talked about me. They treated him like family. I had a good time that night. We didn't get home until four o'clock that morning. I could see why Travis looked forward to Mondays. I acquired more understanding of him and his situation. Also, I began to complain less and cooperate more. I even became more passive. This was opposite from the dominant attitude I once had from being reared by a single, strong, black female.

It was New Year's Eve. We were, once again, in Chicago. This was Travis's and my "partying spot." We flew in on a Tuesday at four o'clock in the afternoon. Belinda was waiting for us at the airport. She took us to the Marriott Hotel on the North-side of Chi-town. We reserved a room when we made the flight arrangements. Tarus and his girlfriend, Christine, were waiting for us. A few other people whom we had met on our last trip to Chicago were there, also. As soon as we got to the hotel, Tarus was waiting for us in the lobby, holding a bag with a bottle of liquor in his hand. We knew it was time to get down.

We checked in, then went upstairs to our room on the eighteenth floor. It was about six-thirty at this time. I looked outside, and saw one of the most invigorating scenes I'd seen in a long time. It was snowing. I'd only witnessed it approximately five times in the past.

Travis said, "Wow, it's been a long time since I've seen snow on New Year's Eve."

I walked over and stood next to him and said, "Isn't it beautiful?" We looked at each other, laughed, and kissed.

TARUS then said, "Alright you two lovebirds, let's have a drink."

About ten o'clock we got dressed and headed downstairs to the ballroom. This is where we were bringing in the New Year. The ballroom was full of people. All of the people that Tarus and Belinda were affiliated with got together and planned this New Year's celebration. I really don't have to elaborate on the balance of the evening, because you already know that we partied the New Year in.

About two o'clock New Year's morning, Travis, Tarus, Belinda, Christine, and a few of their friends all came to our room. We continued to drink, and "Jone"(crack) on each other for hours. We woke up the next morning and called our parents to wish them a Happy New Year. We went back to Tarus's house that day, stayed in Chi-town another day. Then left for home.

Chapter IX

Above the Law

Though Travis was still considered a rookie, he was receiving commendations as well as letters of excellence for the good things he did at work. He was a hell of a police officer. Everyone wanted him as a partner. He was always going "to the rescue" when someone put in a "Help" call. Yet, his level of stress was high. It wasn't coming from home as much as it was from patrolling the streets or the politics he faced in the department. He became the "black-sheep" in his department. This stemmed from speaking his mind at work with his supervisors. In a military-minded regime, tactics and propaganda are not to be under-minded. Yet, if Travis thought that a certain task would jeopardize him or others, he would mention it. For example, at this time, the entire department was understaffed and unfortunately there was not enough manpower on the streets. On occasions his department head ordered two officers to police the projects on foot-beat one night, anyway. In dangerous situations like this, Travis always voiced his opinions. They thought of him as the tyrant that "hell raised." He wasn't as brutally opinionated and honest as his cousin, Tarus, but when it came to his job he wasn't far from it. I was an "ear" every time he wanted to discuss his anger or disgust with whatever was taking place at work.

Travis told me that incidents such as the Rodney King beating made his job tougher, because people were watching and baiting him more. During the Rodney King incident, a year after Travis graduated they rioted downtown in our city. Travis was behind the riot lines watching the crowd as they smashed the windows and looted the stores. Police took no stand.

Before seeing the law enforcement tapes of the Rodney King incident, which incorporated the beatings of Rodney and the incidents that lead up to his beating, Travis immediately took a negative stand. Yet, after he viewed the tape of the Rodney King incident in its entirety, he was more in agreement with what occurred. I WAS SHOCKED WHEN MY HUSBAND TOLD ME THIS. Yet, as Travis explained it to me further.

"*Candi, I'm not at liberty to discuss the contents of the law enforcement tapes. It's against policies. I can't discuss what I saw on those law enforcement tapes before the officers pulled Rodney King over. **But one has to live in a cop's shoes to understand his view**.* For example, I'm patrolling the street and I notice someone driving a car with a broken taillight. I drive up behind him and put on my blue lights, signaling him to pull to the side of the road to give him a warning. The perpetrator looks in his rearview mirror notices me and starts speeding. I start speeding to keep up with him as well. I'm trying to stay behind him, as I barely miss several accidents. He increases his speed to 100 miles an hour. My adrenaline is pumping 200 miles an hour. In keeping up with him, I almost hit a teenage girl as she is crossing the street in front of me. The perpetrator continues to speed jeopardizing the lives of many people. This chase continues for twenty minutes, as we both avoid killing pedestrians and colliding into other vehicles. I soon managed to block him into a dead end street. He jumps out of the car and starts running. I'm pissed because, almost just killed a little girl. I start running after him. Once the moment of showdown approaches and its him and me, there is no switch to automatically turn off my adrenaline."

"Whew, I see."

Because the general public couldn't relate to his and his coworker's experiences, police societies were put in place to provide unlimited support to officers. Travis wasn't aware of any black police societies until further in his career. Early in his career, in a sixty-five percent black department they were nonexistent. In his opinion it has been detrimental to the black officers of the department. They had no voice.

On the other hand, there are several other societies namely, M.A.P.E.S., who Travis was and still is a member of and whose original mission was to support the officers of Irish descent. Yet, this society knows no bounds and accepts and supports officers all over the country regardless of race, sex, and religion.

Eventually, I started noticing a slight change in his attitude. He became arrogant and less cooperative with others and me. I noticed that, while he was in uniform, he displayed an "I am the shit" type of attitude.

One evening after Travis had just gotten home from an E.J. and I had returned from classes, we decided to pick up something quick to eat from the grocery store. Travis left his uniform on because we were both in a hurry to fill our empty stomachs. After getting our groceries, we went to the checkout counter. The checks were always in both of our names. The young lady totaled up our groceries. Travis proceeded to write the check out. Afterward, the cashier said, "Sir, may I see your driver's license?"

Travis said, “Everything you need is on the check, like I’m going to lie about who I am. Hell, I’m the law.”

“What! Travis, the lady just needs to verify that it’s you!” I said while looking at him as if he’d lost his mind. He then proceeded to show her the driver’s license. I guess he figured everyone should trust him, now.

“Candi, just chill, I’m showing it to her, okay? Calm down, it’s not a big deal, damn.”

He started acting as if his badge exempted him from everything. He became overly arrogant and temperamental at times. He acted as if he was above everyone and everything, because he represented the law. The potential he had of ruining a life, if that person broke the law, gave him power beyond what he could handle, at this time.

Several months into the new year of 1995, Travis received an invitation in the mail from one of his old college friends, Daniel. He was getting married. He and his fiancée lived in Washington D.C. So, Travis and I planned a trip to D.C to attend the wedding. After several months passed, we flew to D.C. My baby was so excited about this trip. He hadn’t seen Daniel since they were in college. In college, Daniel never went to class. Travis, Daniel and their other close friends drank a case of beer every day. Their time in college consisted of girls, liquor or beer, and playing sports. Of course they squeezed in a little time for studying, but not much. Travis told me that they were all “buck wild.” All I heard from two weeks to the actual day we departed for D.C. was, “Yeah, I can’t wait to see Daniel and all the boys. I just can’t wait.”

After we got off the plane in D.C. and rented a car, Travis called Daniel. He met us at a corner food store approximately twenty minutes from the airport. On our way to meet Daniel, Travis reminisced about how he and the guys would come to D.C. on weekends or during their breaks while in school together. As we passed the White House and the Washington Monument, I told him about my trip to DC during my summer vacation at the age of fourteen. I was visiting my mom's girlfriend Paulette.

Every summer while in grammar school, my mother would fly my poodle, Gigi and me to different places. I was either visiting my uncle Deangelo and aunt Lillian in New Jersey, my Aunt Beth in Texas, or Paulette in D.C. She wanted me to experience different places and events. I enjoyed every summer as a teenager.

As we drove up to the corner store that Daniel gave us directions to, we saw a blue Acura. In it was Daniel. Travis drove up to Daniel's car. Travis got out of the car and Daniel got out of his. They both ran up to each other and hugged. They were both excited to see each other, high-fiving for a full minute. Daniel told us to follow him, so he could direct us to the hotel that we were staying at, as we weren't familiar with the area. We got to the hotel and noticed that there weren't any parking spaces available except for the ones a quarter of a mile away. Guests could only park up front at the lobby entrance while unloading their bags. We were going to take a much longer time than that, because we wanted to shower and freshen up. Daniel was taking us to meet his wife to be and then later, Travis would meet his friends at the bachelor party. The limited amount of parking spaces was due to a nightclub located inside the hotel. Most of the nightclub's customers were parked in the spaces closest to the hotel. This was noticeable, as we saw people surrounding the side-door entrance to the club. Travis wasn't happy about this at all.

"How can this hotel let those who weren't guests take up all the good spaces from those who are? They should have a designated section, preferably in the back, for those who are going to the club," he said with a bitter tone.

"Well, Boo-Boo, don't worry about it. It's not a big deal. I don't mind walking after we finish unloading our bags."

"No, I'm going to bitch about it. This shit is ridiculous."

I said to myself, *Oh, Boy*! I knew Travis had a temper, especially at this time. The stress that he held inside from work didn't make me feel at ease. I just hoped that the person he complained to would be kind to him and portray a customer is always right type of attitude. I hoped they let him bitch and didn't feed his anger with their opposition. When we got to the front desk, he asked to see the manager. The attendant said that the manager was on break. With much relief to me, he didn't complain.

Thank God! I thought to myself.

We checked in and went up the escalator to our room. After freshening up and getting dressed, Daniel took us to the house he and his fiancée shared. Daniel introduced us to his future wife. I helped her finish the party favors for the wedding to be held the next day. He and Travis went downstairs. They later called Neal, who also went to school with them and lived in D.C. He came over. What a reunion they had. It wasn't until the next day that all of their college friends would come into town. This didn't stop the bachelor party that was scheduled for that night, though.

A few hours passed, then Travis, Neal, and I left. Before they dropped me off at the hotel, we went to Daniel's parents' house. The party was to start in the basement, then progress to different exotic and dance clubs. The basement of Derrick's parents' house is where all the guys were to meet. If you know about D.C., you know about the basement house parties. This basement was half the size of the house. There was a bar at one end of the basement and a pool table on the other. It was designed like a miniature sports bar. Eventually, ten guys and I were all gathered in his parents' basement. There were plenty of alcoholic beverages. Being reunited with his friends from college, drinking and having a good time was utopia for Travis. I sat by him. I conversed with him, Neal and two of Daniel's other friends. Travis talked about his job with the guys, sharing a few of his experiences. That night he treated me as if I were his trophy.

We had a very good time. I even called Paulette and spoke with her for a few minutes. I told her that we were there for a wedding and that we might come to visit her before we left. When I got off the phone, I continued to enjoy mingling with the guys. Before we left Daniel's parents' house, the guys decided who would drive and who wouldn't. In other words, they decided who would do the heavy drinking and who would be the designated drivers. Travis was not one of the designated drivers.

Later on, the guys followed Travis and me to the hotel to drop the car and me off. The other guys piled in a total of three cars tailing us. When we pulled into one of the hotel's entrances, we noticed, again, that there were no hotel parking spaces available except for the ones one-fourth of a mile away from the hotel. This really wasn't a big deal to me. I didn't mind the exercise of walking to the hotel.

While we were driving around the parking lot anticipating that we'd see a spot closer to the lobby, Travis said, "You know, I didn't get a chance to voice my opinion about the parking problem that they have at this hotel."

"Travis, don't worry about it. Let's park the car back here. You go on and get in Daniel's car. I'll go upstairs to the room. Everything will be okay."

He soon pulled the car up to the front lobby and spoke with a slight slur, "Just wait in the car, damn it. I don't want my wife walking three miles to get to her room at anytime while we are staying here."

The other cars pulled up behind us. I knew he was just one step from being drunk. A few seconds later, Travis got out of the car and proceeded to the lobby.

Neal ran up to the car and said, "Candi, where is your husband going?"

"He went to see a hotel manager about the parking situation. He's pissed off that we may have to park our car a quarter of a mile away, just because the club's clients are taking up all the front spaces. He's going in there to raise hell, Neal. I'm a little concerned, because he is slightly intoxicated. Would one of you go in and make sure everything is okay?"

"All right, baby, don't worry about it. He'll be alright."

Neal walked to the other cars to talk with the guys. One minute later, Neal started walking toward the front lobby entrance. I watched him as he proceeded. Before he could open the door, I saw the door swing open with great force. My heart sank. I couldn't believe what my eyes were seeing. This had to be a dream, because it damn sure wasn't reality. Three police officers were carrying my husband out of the hotel. After clearing their way through the door, they dropped him and vigorously tried to contain him. It took three officers to subdue him. One of the officers used all of his body weight to hold him down, while the other two tried handcuffing him. They had his face perpendicular to the cemented ground.

I ran to the altercation, screamed, and said with a tremble in my voice, "What are you guys doing to my husband?" At this time, Neal grabbed me.

I continued shouting, "Let him go. He's a police officer."

Daniel and the other guys ran to the scene. I heard voices in the background, but I didn't know who was saying what.

"Damn, that's fucked up." A voice yelled with excitement.

I also heard, "You don't fuck with the police around here, cause it doesn't matter who you are."

"Yep, they will lock your ass up if you blink wrong." This came from a voice dripping with sarcasm.

The police officer glanced at me and said, "Ma'am, your husband was displaying disorderly conduct. I don't give a shit what he is or who he is."

"Where are you taking him? Travis, Boo, what did you do? What happened?" Travis didn't utter a word. I turned to Neal, who was still holding me. "Neal, what am I going to do?" I pleaded.

"Don't worry about it," Neal said.

Hell, that's what he said two minutes before they arrested my husband.

One of the guys in the group said, "Man, I'm not in the mood for going out any longer."

Another guy said, "Me either."

Daniel said, "We'll wait for an hour to go and get Travis. It's going to take them that much time to get him processed."

Neal said to me, "I'll stay with you in your room to make sure you are okay."

I wondered to myself: Is it a good idea to let Neal stay with me? Would he try anything with me? Nonetheless, I said, *Okay.* I thought to myself, *Shit, at this point, if he were to try anything with me, I would be able to handle myself.* And even if the situation were to present itself, it would be Travis's damn fault for getting me into this predicament anyway. I couldn't believe we came all the way up here for this shit to happen. This would have been the last thing that I would have expected to transpire. Was Travis that drunk? Or was he just pushing his badge around demeaning the people he went to complain to? I know, he was trying to show off. Or maybe he was extremely stressed out from work…so stressed out that he should seek counseling. Hell, at this point I was convinced all of the above had to be true.

It was decided that Neal would wait with me in the hotel room, while Daniel and one of his other friends picked Travis up. So, Neal and I headed up to the room. We conversed about a little of everything…our families, how Travis and I met, etc. There were double beds in the room. I was lying on one of the beds and he was on the other. He made himself comfortable.

"Candi, so what attracted you to your husband?" He asked this with obvious curiosity.

"I met him while out clubbing in Lauderdale. Before long, he started pestering me to go out with him. I didn't think he was my type. Well, I thought he was a square. Despite this I eventually went out and fell in love with him. Now, I realize that he is far from a square. Maybe that was his little ploy; I don't know. With all this shit going on, it seems like I'm the damn square. I guess I had it backwards. But he is a sweetheart, despite his temper."

Neal then said, "You don't look like a married woman."

LET'S BREAK FOR A LITTLE BACKGROUND...Travis always told me I had flirtatious ways. The way that I walked and dressed he'd say was "Not that of a married woman." Yes, I always dressed in somewhat revealing clothes. I always worked hard to keep my body in shape, too. I figured if you got it, flaunt it. That's what my motto was. I also admit that my walk was sexy, but what in the hell was he talking about? This is what, initially, attracted him to me. Maybe I did give guys the wrong impression, but this isn't what I intended to do. Upon first impression, people would say that I didn't look married. I tell you what... I damn sure didn't want to look like some of the married women that I knew of at that time. After two and three years, some of them would just let their bodies go, not caring about their appearance any longer. I guess they figured, "I got what I want" and there is no need to keep their appearance intact. They felt that they weren't on the singles' market any longer, so why should make an effort at looking as good as they looked when their relationship was new. I felt differently about this. I figured the same thing it took to get him was the same thing that it would take to keep him, whether it was appearance, sex, attitude, or personality. Two weeks after I had gotten married, my cousin Annabelle told me the following, "Baby, don't start anything in your marriage that you can not continue or finish." BACK TO THE STORY.

I replied, "If you mean because of how I'm dressed and the sex appeal I have, it's a part of me. I've been looking and dressing like this for a long time. It's just me." After I said this he came over to my bed and sat next to me.

I looked at him and said, "What are you doing?"

He then moved his face closer to mine and tried kissing me. I slowly started easing my body away from him.

"Neal, I can't do this to Travis." I do admit, I was attracted to his caring ways. He seemed concerned about me and how I was feeling as a result of the situation Travis had placed us in. But this kind and caring fashion could have been his plan for getting me into bed. Who knows and, at that point, who cared? I sure didn't.

"Neal, please. Don't do this."

So he stopped and then said, "Okay, sorry. I really wasn't thinking."

He was thinking, all right…thinking about fucking me! I replied, "That's okay. Just don't do that again."

He stayed over for about thirty minutes more. We watched television during this time. He then said, "I need to leave. I'm running late. I should have been over my girlfriend's house an hour ago. I know she's worried about me."

Well, why in the hell was he over here? I couldn't believe him. Then again, I could. He actually thought he was going to get some pussy…and from his old college buddy's wife, while his girlfriend is waiting for him to come over. Men!

Two hours after Neal left, Travis walked into the room. I was in the bed, but not asleep. We both looked at each other, waiting for the other person to speak.

"Candi, I can't believe you didn't come and pick me up."

"Look, you got yourself into this shit. So I figured you can get yourself out of it…Travis, what is wrong with you? You are like dynamite waiting to explode. Am I stressing you out or is it the job? Sweetheart, let me know. Maybe you should go to counseling. What is it? Whatever it is, you are driving me crazy. You are too wild."

"Candi, I'm so sorry that everything happened the way it did. I ruined the bachelor party, ruined the trip, and embarrassed my wife."

Tears ran down his face. My poor baby surely did need help. God, I felt so bad for him. For someone who was extremely upset, I surely didn't have anger for him any longer. I felt sorry for him. My, how quickly my emotions changed from one extreme to the other.

"I'm not going to the wedding," he said.

"Travis, no, we are going to the wedding. We didn't fly here for the hell of it. Everyone makes mistakes. I'll be by your side, so don't worry about it. We'll stick this out together." I didn't dare tell him about the stunt that Neal pulled.

The following day, we met everyone, the bridal party as well as Daniel's friends and family at the church for the wedding. As soon as Travis and I stepped out of the car, I began to feel uncomfortable. I had a feeling that everyone would be talking about what happened the night before. As we walked up the stairs of the church, I looked to my right and saw one of the guys who was with us the night before. He was whispering to someone while looking at us. I know that if I were embarrassed, I couldn't begin to imagine how Travis felt. Humility had engulfed my husband's face. If I had a magic wand, I would have made the twenty-four hours that day, feel like one fleeting minute.

The wedding was beautiful. So was the bride. It had been one of the most well planned weddings that we had been to. Everything was perfect. At the reception, things felt better to us. There were twice as many people at the reception than at the wedding. There were at least three hundred guests. There was plenty of food, displayed banquet style. Eventually, one and one-half hours into the wedding reception the fellas and I joked with Travis a bit about what had happened. Most of them felt that he was out of his mind, but also, they knew how the police in that town overreacted at times. After the reception, half of the guests went back to Daniel's parents' home. There we ate like gluttons, stuffing our faces with fried fish, potato salad, tossed salad, rolls, and dessert. We always ate a lot on trips. That night we enjoyed ourselves so much, we forgot about everything even the incident the night before. The next day, we left for home.

Chapter X

Shattered Hearts

A few months after the D.C. incident, I decided to go to a party that a few of my coworkers were throwing. It was one of the best parties that I'd been to. They sold tickets to the party to raise money to provide unlimited amounts of food and drinks for their guests. Their spread consisted of steak, chicken, fish, shrimp, beans, potato salad, meatballs,...ohhh, the list went on. I was especially happy because I could drink all of the zinfandel and mixed drinks I wanted. The music was great. Everything was well done. The party started at eight o'clock this night. Travis came with me, but later left at ten-thirty to go to work. One of my coworkers introduced me to this guy named Keith, one of his longtime friends. Keith and I talked for a few minutes about the party, but nothing more. Soon we went our separate ways and continued partying.

On the next working day, my phone started ringing at work. I answered the phone with a greeting and heard Keith's voice on the other end, "Hey, Candi. How are you? This is Keith."

I thought he was cute, but I wasn't really interested in him. "Hi, Keith. What's up?"

"Well, I thought I would call to say Hi and touch base with you."

"Really?"

"Yeah"

"Well, I'm married, Keith, and how did you get my phone number anyway?"

"Sexy, I already know that you are married…and to a cop at that. Your coworker, my boy, gave me your number. Look, I just want you to know that I was thinking about you. I checked you out at the party. I dig your style. You are so damn sexy."

I do admit, this felt good to hear. Travis didn't compliment me often, so I enjoyed hearing other men tell me this.

"Well, thanks," I said. Hell, what was the harm in conversing with him? I felt that I needed this ego boost any damn way. This felt good for some reason. Usually, guys told me that I looked good enough to eat and that I was a sexy individual, but most comments never penetrated my emotional being.

"Well, you aren't so bad looking yourself," I said.

"Thanks. So, do you mind if I call you every now and then?"

"No, you can call me every now and then." I had to repeat his question in my answer, because I didn't want this motherfucker calling me every single day.

"Okay, well, I'm just touching bases with you. If you want to call me sometime, dial 555-9043 or you can page me at 555-9870."

I wrote the numbers down and we both hung up.

Several weeks later, while at work, Travis called me. He wanted me to look for an incident report in his duffel bag located in the trunk of the car that I had taken to work that day. He needed information from this report. I had taken the car he'd driven the previous day. We switched cars regularly. Many times he did not remove his belongings from one car to another. So, I took a break and went out to the car. I started searching and searching. Soon I found a yellow enveloped marked "Internal Affairs" with date of two days prior. I opened it. It was the statement that Travis had given to Internal Affairs about the incident that took place at BB's. I paused for a second to decide if I should read it. I thought to myself, I would be wrong for reading it, because it will invade his privacy, but why didn't he mention to me that he received the report two days ago? Maybe it was my business, then again maybe it wasn't. I decided to read the transcript, which follows:

Internal Affairs Official: So who were you with the night that this occurred?

Officer Dixon: There were three of us, me, Officer Derrick Dean, and Officer Winston Walker.

Internal Affairs Official: Were you guys with anyone else?

Officer Dixon: Yes, we were with three other girls. One of which I met at a park….

I don't believe this. I don't believe it. I just know he wasn't with another female. I said to myself, panicking. I continued to read:

Officer Dixon: Her name was Sheila. She went with us to BB's after we left the park.

Internal Affairs Official: Did you know her before tonight?

Officer Dixon: No, I'd just met her that night.

OPS Official: If we need to get in contact with her for a statement, do you have her number?

Officer Dixon: Yes. Her number is… After reading the number, I wrote it down. I, then, said to myself *Oh, Hell, no. I'm leaving this son-of-a lying bitch. Oh, No….* I felt myself becoming hysterical. I raced back into my office and called the number that I'd just written down.

"Hello," a squeaky voice answered the phone.

"Yes, hello, this is Travis Dixon's wife, soon to be ex-wife. Do you remember him?"

"Travis, Dixon...let me see, Travis Dixon…ooh yea, I remember him. Light skinned, big guy."

"Yes, that's him. I..."

She cut me off and said, "Oh yeah, he was the one fighting at BB's. He's a funny and nice person", she said pleasantly.

"Well, was he trying to flirt or talk to you? Your name and number are in the statement that he gave Internal Affairs."

"Oh, no, he wasn't. As a matter of fact, we knew he was married. There were two other women with me. We followed one of the girls to meet her boyfriend at the park. Her boyfriend was with your husband and several other guys. That's when we all, as a group, decided to go to BB's. It was innocent. Travis did not try to talk to me. I don't know how he got my number, though. I never gave it to him."

"Oh, well, I'm sorry if I disturbed you. I had to get to the bottom of this to make sure that my husband wasn't cheating on me," I said feeling slightly relieved, but not totally.

"Oh, don't worry about it. I understand." I hung up and sighed with relief. Still, I was disappointed in Travis. He never told me that women were in their company. I called Travis up.

"Hello," he said.

"Look, I thought we agreed to start being honest and open with each other. You are a lying sack of shit, Travis." I totally forgot about the information he wanted me to get, originally.

"What are you bitching about now? Damn. What is the problem?"

"I'm not bitching. Why didn't you tell me that you guys were at BB's with women?"

"Because, I really wasn't with any women, per se. The girls that you are probably talking about were with Winston's girlfriend. And Winston was with us. Candi, I wasn't with any girl in particular. It was a group thing."

"A group thing? What in the world do you mean by a group thing?"

"You know what I mean. Oh, girl, nobody is messing around on you all right? I just didn't think it was a big deal to mention, that's all."

Yeah right. He thought it was a big enough deal to mention it to Internal Affairs. He was just insecure about mentioning other women to me, whether he wanted them or not. That's all this was.

"And where did you get her number from, if you weren't dealing with her? Come on, really, Travis," I said in disbelief, but I felt the opposite.

I felt that he wasn't involved with her, but I was upset with him because he was dishonest with me. He hadn't mentioned anything about females the night of that incident.

"Winston and I had already planned what we would say. He got the number from his girlfriend and gave it to me. His girlfriend was a friend of Sheila's, the one I mentioned in my statement. And the reason we even mentioned them in the statement is that we didn't want Internal Affairs to think we were just out among the fellas getting drunk and causing trouble. We wanted them to know that women were in our company and that we weren't trying to cause any problems."

I ended up giving him the information that I had originally gone out to the car to look for, before I stumbled upon that statement. We talked for a bit longer; then we hung up. I felt betrayed, still. He never mentioned the details about the women they were with that evening. Hell, even if I wanted to trust him, he was making it awfully difficult for me to do so. There was simply no reason for him to conceal those facts. It was unnecessary. I would have understood. At this point I figured if he concealed this shit, then he would conceal other things from me. This did not help our relationship as far as the important element of trust was concerned.

At this point, what kept us together was the grace of God. I didn't trust Travis and he didn't trust me. Elements that held the stitches together in the relationship were the nightly dining together, the praying together and the deep (sometimes hidden) love that that we shared for one another. If it weren't for those things, we wouldn't have made it to this point. When the "ups" reached a heightened point, the "downs" would inevitably come forth, bringing the relationship below an equilibrium point.

It was Thanksgiving. Frank's parents invited us over to dine with them. They told us to bring some barbecue beef ribs. Barbecue Beef ribs? I wondered where that would fit into the Thanksgiving dinner. Yet, I thought to myself, today people serve non-traditional as well as traditional entrées for the holidays. Nonetheless, I cooked the ribs in beer sauce on slow heat for seven hours. They were delicious. When I sampled one of the ribs, I almost ate my damn fingers off. The meat was well seasoned and so tender it fell off of the bone.

When we got over to Frank's parents' home, I socialized with Sierra, Frank's girlfriend then. She was from our hometown, also. She visited Frank every now and then. Suspicious of Frank and his infidelity, she knew that he was up to no good, yet she still loved him. Sierra and I stayed upstairs in Frank's room most of the afternoon. Mutual friends of Travis' and Frank's were there, also. Most of the evening the guys stayed in a room downstairs. Everyone was single, except for Frank's parents as well as Travis and me. (While living in Georgia, we knew very few couples.) Travis came upstairs every now and then to kiss me and see how I was doing.

That evening, Sierra and I joined everyone downstairs to eat dinner. At dinner, we ate a feast…turkey, ham, dressing, candied yams, potato salad, several casserole dishes, tossed salad, collard greens, sweet potato soufflé, my beef ribs, desserts and much more. Sierra and I laughed at the dressing. We didn't know who made it, but the shit was awful. The rest of the food, for the most part, was good.

Sierra and I went back upstairs after eating. Frank always wanted Travis to go places with him. A few times he'd go, but most of the times he didn't. At this time I was feeling more insecure than ever, due to the problems that we had faced in the past. Travis may have had more trust in me than I did in him, but neither one of us thoroughly trusted the person. At about nine o'clock that evening, Travis came upstairs to the room that Sierra and I were in.

"Baby, me and the fellas are getting ready to go to the liquor store and ride around for a minute."

Hell, the way I saw it, this was Thanksgiving and there was really no reason for a married man to be out riding in the streets, chasing the "happenings." He should be with his loved one(s). ***Today, both of us would have surely handled things differently than the way we did.***

"What in the world do you need to go hangin' with them for? It's the holidays and you should be here with me."

"I won't be long. We should be back in an hour."

"Travis, I don't think you are going."

"Oh, yes I am. Why are you making a big deal of this?"

"Look, quite often, it's all about the boys. Shit I get sick of the boys."

He then left the room as if he didn't care and started walking down the stairs.

I soon grabbed the car keys from of my purse and told Sierra, "Girl, I don't need this shit. I'm calling somebody up and getting out of here. The boys this and the boys that…He needs to marry the damn boys."

Sierra said, "Girl, you know how they are."

Then she started walking toward the bathroom. I headed downstairs, while she was in the bathroom. I went outside and got into our car. Soon, the guys started coming outside. Travis's gun was in his hand. He had just picked it up from where he and the guys were sitting inside the house. He was getting ready to put his gun inside his shirt, when he saw me inside the car.

He came up to the car with the gun in his hand and said, "Where do you think you are going?"

"I'm getting the hell out of here. We came over here to spend the holiday together, not apart."

"Well, I'm just making a run with the boys."

"Well, you go make it. I'm leaving."

My window was up, all this time. I wasn't about to let it down. It was cold, plus I hadn't planned on carrying on a conversation with him, anyway. While he was talking, I started backing the car up. My foot was on the brake pedal and the car was in neutral. The car had a stick shift. He decided to get behind the car. I slightly lifted my foot off of the brake pedal, so that the car would slowly back up. The driveway was on a slight hill. Travis started backing up with the car.

As he backed up with the car, he said, "Candi, stop this damn car. You aren't going anywhere."

I continued backing the car up. He backed up with the car. The car was rolling back very slowly. Soon he moved from behind the car to my side, the driver's side. He started tapping the butt of the gun against the car door window. It was apparent that he wasn't trying to break it. If he were, he would have immediately used greater force.

"Candi, stop the car. You don't need to go anywhere. Stay here. I won't be gone long…."

I, at this time, thought that he was out of his mind. Why was he using the butt of the gun to knock on the window? He should know the hazards of doing this. He should have been using his hands to knock on the window. Actually, he shouldn't have knocked on the window at all. Before he could finish what he was saying, the butt's metal piece of the gun hit the window and shattered glass everywhere. I was in shock. Now we could work through the other problems, but I knew we weren't going to work through this.

What in the hell was he thinking? He had broken the window. OOOOh, I felt so embarrassed, lifeless and humiliated. Glass was in the car and all over my clothes. Luckily, I wasn't hurt, though I could have been. A few fragments of glass hit my ear, leaving a few red spots. They were gone the next day, fortunately. Travis, as I found out later, had a few cuts on his hand. I didn't know at the time because I never got out of the car to see. I know he didn't mean to shatter the window, because had he wanted to he would have forcefully shoved the gun into the glass. But why in the world would he use his gun to tap the window? As I backed into the street, I turned the wheel of my car, so that the car could be parallel with the street. I placed the car in first gear and got the hell out of there.

For the first time in our relationship, I didn't want to see him anymore. I really meant it. I he thought of him made my stomach turn. His gun had no place in that situation. I drove home to our apartment and called his father.

I can't tell you why I called his father, but maybe it was because I figured an authority figure, one whom he deeply respected and deeply admired, needed to talk to him. So I told his father what had happened. His father ended up calling him over Frank's mother's house. The guys who were with Travis told Frank's mother that I tried running Travis over. Hell, if I were going to run the son of a bitch over, I would have stepped on the gas. He would have had tire marks over his body. He also would have been parallel to the ground. There would have been no question as to whether I did or didn't. Those who thought I ran him over can believe whatever they want. I know what I did and what my intentions were. I wasn't a violent person. I just didn't have a problem telling people exactly how I felt. Maybe they confused the two. I could never run him over, even if I wanted to. Because Frank's mother told Travis's father the misleading information,

Travis's father figured that we both were wrong about the incident. He never got a chance to talk to Travis because they left to go to the liquor store. There was no question in my mind that he needed help. I knew I wasn't going to stick around and put up with him under these conditions. I just needed to figure out how I would leave him. We didn't have enough money in the bank so that I could get an apartment of my own. Also, I was too embarrassed by this entire incident to tell any of two or three friends that I did have, so I didn't feel comfortable staying with any of them.

A half an hour after speaking with Travis' father, I called Sandy at Frank's parents' house. "Sierra, it's me, Candi," I said.

"Girl, what in the world just happened?" she said with a loud, excited tone.

"Well, I left like I said I was going to. Travis told me that he didn't want me to leave. I ignored him, got in the car, and started backing the car up. He got behind the car, then came to the driver's side and broke the car door window with the butt of his gun. Girl, he had the gun in his hand when he was coming from inside of the house. He'd just picked it up from the countertop of the room they were in downstairs. He started to put the gun in his pants, but didn't after he saw me in the car. I don't know what he was thinking. I don't know if he forgot to put the gun in his pants after seeing me or if he was trying to show off with it. Sierra, I want to leave, but I have no money and no place to go. I know he didn't mean to break the window, but the fact is, it broke anyway. If people only knew what kind of individuals are protecting their city."

Sierra then said, "Girl, they just got back. You should see the look on Travis's face. Agony was written all over it. I went downstairs. Apparently, after all this took place, the guys were loudly talking about what had happened. I looked at Travis. He was in another zone. He was in shock. He hasn't said a word since."

"Well, that's not my business, now," I said.

"Girl, I'll be over there in a minute." Frank's parents lived fifteen minutes away.

Sierra came over. Presently, she and Frank were having problems, too. Nonetheless, she comforted me and told me accidents happen.

"Candi, you should be pissed, but accidents do occur. You know Travis wouldn't try to hurt you."

"Yes, but he broke my window. I could have been hurt as well. He also embarrassed me and caused a big scene."

"But you weren't hurt."

We talked for a while; then decided to get a hotel room. I told her that I didn't want to stay here and see Travis's face when he walked in the door. I told her that I couldn't stand the sight of him at the time.

"Girl, you know they said you ran him over."

"Sierra, I was just slowly letting the car roll back. If I tried running Travis over, he would have been in the hospital by now, because I would have stepped on the gas. For several seconds, he continued to back up as I let the car roll slowly. If that's what they mean by running him over, then I guess I did."

We got a room at the hotel and talked until nearly sunrise. Then, we slept for a few hours.

She decided to stay in the room with me that night because she needed a break from Frank. She was tired of Frank's lies about the women that were calling him. After a few hours of sleep, I woke up. A sense of calm and peace filled me, as if I were drifting on soft, white clouds surrounded by a heavenly spring atmosphere. All of a sudden, I was drawn into dirty, dark memories torturing me about what had just occurred. I said to myself, *it's a just dream*. As I looked at my surroundings, at the other bed and saw Sierra, I knew that it wasn't a dream. This was real.

Maybe these weren't major problems to some people, but they were to me. I was raised in a strict, sheltered environment and thought the world of marriage would be like a fairy tale. My mother always shielded me from the harsh realities of the world. Yes, I partied with my friends back at home, but I never ran into people with major relationship problems. At least they never told me about them. I was an unbelievably naïve person with serious marital problems. Until I started having problems, my mother never told me about the things that some married couples went through, such as the inability to resolve conflict, domestic violence, infidelity, jealousy, spouses that bailed their mates out of jail and babies conceived outside of the marriage. Why didn't she tell me what I was potentially in store for? Did only a few married people experience minor problems or did every couple have major problems that were minimized by how they looked at their problems or solved them? I knew that my husband and I were extremely jealous and insecure about each other and ourselves when we got married. Yet, the number of issues we needed to both work on made the list infinite.

While at the hotel, I called my mom. And, unfortunately, she was not there. She was in Las Vegas. After I got her answering machine recording, I remembered that she told me that she'd be in Vegas on Thanksgiving weekend.

Sierra and I decided to eat breakfast at the Waffle House. When we got there we seated ourselves. The waitress came to our table and asked us what we wanted to drink. We told her that we would order our food and drinks because both of us had already talked about what we'd order on the way there. Sierra ordered a patty melt, hash browns and orange juice. I ordered a pecan waffle, grilled chicken breast, hash browns, and orange juice.

After the waitress took our order and left, I said, "Sierra, don't you think that this justifies me leaving him?"

"Girl, no. Does he mistreat, beat, or physically and mentally hurt you? This shit was an accident, Candi."

"No, hell no, he doesn't physically beat me, but we are harsh with our words to each other."

"Girl, please. Travis is a good person. He seems to have a temper, but you don't want to leave him just because he broke your driver's side window. You sound stupid and dumb as hell. I know you are pissed, 'cause I would be pissed, too, but you need to let him know this and carry on. Shit, if you think that his temper is a real problem, go see a counselor. Girl, leave him over something that makes sense, okay?"

I laughed and said, "Well, maybe you are right, but Sierra, this really scared me."

"I know! You guys need to work through this. I've seen a whole hell of a lot worse than this between couples and they stick together. That's if they really love each other. Ain't nobody perfect. Maybe he's stressed out on the job. Shit, I'd go nuts, too, if I daily had to fuck around with all those crazy ass people out there. Girl, Travis has a tough job…and his life is even more complicated if you guys have problems."

"I hear ya. What about you and Frank?"

"Well, I'm going to leave him. I've been thinking about this for a while. He's up here and I'm down in Florida. I am tired of his lies about the women that call for him. I know fucks everyone when I'm in Florida. Besides, Frank and I aren't on the same page anymore. He ain't trying to get his own life together. What does it look like? Me...get with him so that we can live with his momma? I don't think so. He can't keep a job, so, how in the hell is he going to help with the bills? No, Candi, I don't think so. Shit, at least Travis works, and two jobs sometimes at that."

"Sierra, are you serious about Frank?"

"Candi, I am as serious as a heart attack. I don't want him anymore. I need someone responsible in my life. He is not it. Really, Candi."

A few minutes later, the waitress brought our food. We ate and went back to the hotel room. She called Frank and told him that she would be there soon. They talked for a minute and then hung up.

"Candi, you know we have to be out of this room at two o'clock." We both looked at the clock. It was one-thirty. She continued, "It's time for us to go home. Yes, you need to go home. It's messed up that he broke the window, but it's not the end of the world." She yelled, "HE MADE A MISTAKE!"

I knew she was tired of me, but she was the only person I could talk to at this time. Sierra and I had gotten to know each other through Frank. She would come up to visit him every now and then. She, at one time, even thought about moving here. She changed her mind, though, because she thought the relationship's future was non-existent. I was a little disappointed, because we started to become very close.

She continued. "Look, girl, go home. You guys really need to talk about this. So, get your things and let's go."

Sierra didn't mind being honest about anything. So, I listened to what she said and left the hotel with her. We'd driven separate cars. She went home. I didn't go home after I left the hotel room. Travis's working hours were 11 p.m.-7 a.m. So, I decided to kill time and wait for Travis to leave for work at ten o'clock that night. By now, it was only three o'clock, so, I had seven hours to kill. I still wasn't interested in facing him. I heard what Sierra had said, but I still didn't know if I wanted him any longer. I went to the mall, movies, and dinner. This took every bit of seven hours.

It was ten-thirty p.m. when I decided to go home. By now, I thought to myself, he'd be gone. I figured I could go home and continue thinking about what to do in this situation. As soon as I pulled up to our apartment building, I noticed that his car was still there. Why was he still home? *Damn*, I said to myself. I decided to go inside and face the music. I walked in the door. He was sitting on the sofa. The television was on and so was our stereo. He was in a daze. He didn't even hear me come in. I passed the sofa that he was sitting on to go in our bedroom.

Before I could get into the room, he put his arm in my path, held out his hands and said, with a soft voice, "Candi, dear, could you please come here?"

I maneuvered around his arm and said, "Don't you put your nasty-ass hands on me. Don't touch me. Don't look at me."

"You stayed out all night. You weren't even concerned about me, Candi. I even hurt my hand."

Just as I thought he was out of his mind for asking me to take him to dinner when we first met, I thought the same when he said this. Why would I be concerned about someone who obviously didn't use good judgment about what he'd done and one who embarrassed us in front of all those people? He was insane. After that remark he made, I was eager to talk to him and let him have it.

"Look, I don't even know who you are…you broke the car door window in front of all those people. You could have hurt me. I was totally embarrassed and I can't believe you have the audacity to think that I should be concerned about you. Go TO HELL!"

"Look, you tried to run me over. And you know I didn't mean to break the window. You know that."

"I don't know anything anymore. And another thing, you need to stop letting those fuckin' raggedy-ass people over there, put information in your head like that. If I wanted to run you over, I would have left tire marks all over your body. You would have been left for dead. I'm not like that and I wasn't raised in this kind of environment, either. This is not the kind of shit that I am used to. I'm scared. I don't even know who you are."

"Dear, please. I was tapping the butt of the gun on the window. Then the metal piece of the butt hit the window and shattered the glass. You know I didn't mean to do that. Yes, I was very upset with you, because I thought you tried to run me over. You also had no reason to leave, just because I was leaving. I told you that we would be back. I wouldn't try hurting you or disrespecting you because we all know that *Candi will get her things and leave. You always run out the door to escape any problems we have. Be a woman and not a little fuckin' girl.* Face up to the problems we have and let's try solving them. Hell, every time I look around you are packing your bags. You know I would not intentionally try to hurt the queen. Please, cut it out, Candi. You are acting ridiculous now."

He was telling the truth. I really didn't want to admit it. This wasn't about me, though. It was about him. This still didn't erase the fact that he was wrong. How was he going to control his temper and use good judgment while he was angry? Then I started thinking to myself: *why is he still home*? Hell, I wanted to call my mother and talk to her privately. I needed her opinion about this situation.

"What are you doing home?"

"Well, I couldn't work because I didn't know where you were. I couldn't concentrate until we talked. I want to be with my wife. I don't want to lose you."

"Well, you just may, if you keep this up."

"And where were you? Who were you with?"

"That's none of you business." I knew he would find out later from Frank. When Sierra spoke with Frank at the hotel, she told him where we were. When Travis and I went to bed that night, I didn't let him touch me. I was still disgusted with him.

The next day, I didn't speak to him at all. Despite everything, he was the sweetest gentleman that one could be. He prepared breakfast for me, bathed me, and helped me put my clothes on. He was like a servant. Later that night, he went to work. I couldn't wait to locate my mother in Vegas. I didn't know what hotel she was in, so I started calling all over the city to the different major hotels, until I found her. I finally discovered she was staying at the Mirage Hotel. I was so happy that I'd found her. She wasn't in her room at the time that I called, so I left a message for her at the front desk.

A few hours later, I heard the phone ringing. I knew it was her calling me back.I answered the phone by saying, "Ma, is this you?"

"Yes, Candi, it's me." She said with a surprising tone, "What's wrong?"

"Oh, Ma, you can't imagine what Travis has just done to me. I can't believe this happened. I think it's time for me to leave him, Ma."

By this time, she was anxious for me to get to the point.

"Candi, what happened?" she said with slight fear of how tragic the news I was getting ready to tell her would be.

"Mommy…," I started whining. "Travis broke the car door window, while I was in the car. He was tapping on the window with his gun, while I was backing up. When the metal portion hit the window, the glass shattered. I could have been hurt. He said he didn't mean to do it, but I don't care. I was and still am so embarrassed. He was trying to go somewhere with his friends for an hour or so, but I told him he needed to stay at the house with me. This happened in front of several people. We were at Frank's mom's house. I just don't know what to do. I am furious about the incident and at Travis. Ma, shouldn't I leave him?"

I always looked for a confirmation from my mother. I realized that I needed to grow up. Travis was right about that. I felt that her word was "THE WORD." No one else's opinion mattered. I deeply respected my mother and feared what she'd think and say at times. Maybe that's why I didn't want to live with Travis without being married. After I grew up, she told me to do what I wanted to do and she meant it, yet I knew how she felt about it. Strict with me, yet wild with her friends, she shielded a lot from me and told me that a lot of things that went on in her life and her friends' lives were not for a little girl's eyes or ears. I have an unexplainably deep respect for her morals, but shielding me from reality made me ridiculously naïve. A hell of a job ya' did ma, though.

"Candi, is it me or is it you? First of all, you don't need to worry about what others think of you. And secondly, do you really think he meant to break the window? Candi, my grandmother used to always say 'Teeth and tongue will fall out'. This means that no matter how close you are, there will be problems. You two are different people with different personalities. So, problems are inevitable. Now, if he was mistreating you, honey, I would surely understand your frustration, but he treats you good. Now, he may have a temper problem, but you guys should go to counseling. And you're not perfect, either, Candi."

"Ma, do you think so?"

As my ignorance surfaced I continued, "Have you heard of couples going through situations worse than what we just went through…yet, they are still together?"

"Oh, God, where did I go wrong with my child?" she said in frustration. "Candi, this ain't shit compared to some of the things that people go through. Look, Attorney Brown got some chick pregnant while he was married. He and his wife are still together. The child is even grown now. They didn't get a divorce. I'm not saying that they should or shouldn't have, but they decided to stick it out. Now, don't you think that is worse than your situation? That's not even the beginning of the things that people go through. Also, it's what the two people in the relationship are willing to accept. Candi, surely you can't be this naïve?"

"Ma, you were strict. Of course, I am learning about life now, more than ever, since I've been married."

"That's what you always tell me. I guess I was a horrible mother."

"Ma, stop, you know I didn't mean that."

"Candi, if you guys do anything, go see a counselor. You don't need to leave him over this. It doesn't merit that."

"Thanks, Ma, I really appreciate it."

"That's what mothers are for."

"Well, enjoy the rest of your trip. By the way, have you enjoyed it thus far? I'm so caught up in my dilemma that I forgot to ask you about it."

"Roomy and I are having a good time. Missy, it has been really nice. Tomorrow, we are supposed to fly over the Grand Canyon." Roomy was a nickname that she had given her girlfriend and high school classmate, Mae Ida. They had a lot in common such as one kid, being divorced, the same age, and still trying to date. They traveled the country together a lot, also.

"Okay."

"Bye, I love you, Ma."

"I love you, too, Candi."

Yes, I felt a little better after talking with my mother and getting her feedback. Life just couldn't go on unless I knew it was okay with my mother. There were a few times that I would say, "the hell with what she thinks," but for the most part I had to get her approval.

Eventually, I decided not to leave Travis. For what…? So someone else could enjoy his cooking, washing clothes, and caring ways? On the other hand, I damn sure didn't want to stay through all this shit he was putting me through, either. *Travis was too good to leave and too bad to stay with.* Did I really cause some of this, because of my nagging and bitching? I was so damn confused at the time. Someone told me, *"Make sure you have done all that you can do to make your marriage work, so if it doesn't, you can walk away with a clear conscience."* I'm not sure who told me this, but I never forgot these words. Well, I knew I wasn't the best wife, so I started trying to be the best I could be…at least at home. If he acted like a fool, I could leave without ever looking back.

Chapter XI

Wandering Eyes

I was confused at the time with all the problems that were prevalent in my marriage. My mind started wandering. I was tired of actually being a good girl. I needed something refreshing, new, and exciting in my life. I didn't know what it was, but I needed it.

While standing outside my office with my manager, finishing a conversation about a manual I needed to create, I heard my phone ringing.

"Okay, Peter, I should have a rough copy of it by 4:00 p.m. tomorrow. Let's set a meeting at 4:15 p.m. tomorrow afternoon to review it," I said rubbing my chin while speaking to my manager.

"Sounds great, Candi," he replied.

As my manager walked away, I went back into my office and answered the phone.

"Hey, sexy." God, I was really glad to hear his voice.

"Hey, Keith. How are you?" Keith was exactly what I had viewed as my type...tall, dark, built, and handsome….a "woman's dream come true."

"Well, lovely lady, just fine."

Hell, I didn't give a shit if he called all of the women he knew "lovely lady"…this felt good to hear. At this point, I was so down and out that a fuckin' toad could have told me I looked good and I would have been excited to hear it from him.

He continued, "I've been thinking about you lately. I know you are married, but that doesn't stop me from thinking about you. We don't have to take this any further than just a friendship, but I would like for us to have a drink together one day. If you are uncomfortable with that, then I will just continue to call you every now and then. Whatever makes you happy, sexy." His tone was soft, but his voice was deep. It sounded so soothing.

"Keith, maybe we can have drinks one day. I'm just unsure of the day. By the way, what do you do for a living?" Before I wasted any more of my time talking to this guy, I wanted to make sure he wasn't earning three dollars and fifty cents an hour.

"I'm a marketing consultant for a large firm in the city." I saw a few dollar signs.

I then said, "So, where did you go to school?"

"I went to Texas State University. I played football there."

"Where are you from?"

"I'm originally from New York."

He seemed to be real down to earth, as well. But why didn't he have anyone at the time? What in the hell was wrong with him?

"Are you seeing someone, now?"

"No, I just got out of a three-year relationship. We were incompatible. We could never communicate. That brings me here. Alone. You listening to me, sexy?"

"Yes," I said.

"I just wanted to make sure. Is that all right with you?"

"I guess."

"Well, you have my phone numbers, so give me a call anytime whenever the urge hits you, okay? I'll leave it to you to let me know when you'd like for us to have a drink."

We hung up after saying our good-byes.

I called him one week later. We continued to learn about each other on the phone. Soon, we began to talk on the phone every couple of days for. This went on for two months Finally, one day I told him that we could meet at a tavern to have a few drinks. I planned it around a time I knew Travis would be at work…approximately eleven-thirty.

The night arrived. He told me on the phone to look for a black Mercedes Benz 300E. I drove to the tavern we decided to meet at. He had gotten there before me. As I pulled up, he got out of his car and came over to mine. He was dressed in a long sleeved black sweater. I could tell he worked out due to the ripples of muscles that were bulging through his shirt. He also had on blue jeans. I started saying to myself, *Travis and I better get our relationship together, because it's going to be all over soon for us*. Keith had on some cologne that would make a virgin throw her panties at him. I could smell his cologne because my window was down. I kept telling myself, be *good, Candi. We are only going to have a drink.*

He opened my car door and said, "Good Evening, sexy. How are you feeling?"

"Fine," I said. I entered into another zone. What in the hell was I doing here? How did I ever get to this point?

"Let me take your hand," he said gallantly. I gave him my hand.

He guided me out of the car. He said, "Watch your step." I got out of the car and locked it. He grabbed me, gently moved me aside, and closed my car door. *Damn, he was a gentleman, too*, I said to myself. We went inside. I told him I wanted to sit at the bar, so we did. He helped me in my seat. He, then, sat in his. The bartender came up to us a few minutes after we sat down. We ordered drinks, and talked for a while. He was a lot of fun and I enjoyed his company. He was easy to talk to. We talked about everything ...college, past relationships, jobs, people in politics, and what turned us off and on, sexually. He never tried anything with me, but he asked me if I would come over to his place. I told him maybe another time, but not that night. After we finished our drinks, he walked me to the car, kissed me on the cheek and said, "Thanks for a beautiful evening."

"No problem, Keith," I said.

"I'll call you tomorrow." He waved his hand as he spoke.

The next day, I was surprised at what I saw as I walked into my office. A dozen pink long stemmed roses were sitting in a vase on my desk. There was a card enclosed in an envelope situated under the vase. I opened it and it read: "Sexy, I really enjoyed our evening last night." There were three X's and three O's at the bottom of the card. I sighed. He made everything seem normal again. The dark clouds in my sky were starting to dissipate. The ton of weights that I'd been carrying mentally had been lifted. He really brightened up my day! I immediately called him at work. He answered his phone.

I then said, "Keith, you didn't have to do this. This was such a sweet gesture. You made me feel so good."

"That's all I want to do. Don't take what I said the wrong way. Now, if just being friends with me feels good to you, then that's all I want us to be. But one thing is for sure, I wish you weren't married."

I said to myself, *I wish I weren't either, sometimes*.

"Keith thanks again. I really felt comfortable around you last night. I felt I could just be myself, say everything on my mind, and talk to you about anything. It was the best time."

"I look forward to more evenings like that, whenever the time is good for you. I don't want to pressure you. I just want to spoil you with my friendship." Whether or not these were "lines" I didn't care. This guy was turning me on. Just then, one of my coworkers came into my office.

"Okay," I said to Keith, "I have to go. I'll call you later." I hung up the phone. I then spoke with my coworker for a few minutes. As soon as my coworker left, my phone started ringing.

I picked it up and said, "Candi Dixon speaking."

"Hey, Scooter, why didn't you call me this morning to see if I was doing okay? You normally call me to make sure that I am okay and say I love you, if you leave the house before I get home in the mornings."

"Well, hey Travis. How are you? I love you," I said with a dull voice. Actually, I was thinking about Keith at this time. I really wasn't interested in talking to Travis at that moment.

"What is wrong with you?" he said, astonished.

"Oh, nothing, baby doll. I'm fine. I'm just a little tired. Are you okay?" I immediately switched my tone of voice.

"Baby, I got a surprise for you when you get home. I got something for my baby." He started singing these words. "I got something for my baby. I got us some tickets to go to the basketball game next Monday."

I thought to myself: Why in hell does he want to start spending time with me going somewhere different than a sports bar on Mondays, now? A part of me didn't want him to miss a Monday with his boys, now. I also wished he would fuck up somehow, so that I could have justification for seeing Keith. I was glad, but disappointed, at the same time.

"Travis, you are welcome to take one of your boys with you. I won't mind."

"No, I'm taking my beautiful wife." Great, he wants me first on Mondays, now. Damn, I was just getting into Keith. It would be hard to get involved with Keith, while Travis was being a total angel.

Travis and I started spending more time with Derrick, his girlfriend, and a few other couples. Derrick sold drugs on the side. His girlfriend was an exotic dancer at a nightclub. We had cookouts every so often, especially on holidays such as the Fourth of July and Memorial Day. Even if we ran out of food, you better believe that there was plenty of liquor.

It was a clear, sunny, spring, Sunday morning. I awoke before Travis. Still lying flat on my back, I started rubbing my feet up and down Travis's right leg. I saw one of his eyes open. One second later his other eye opened.

"Hey, Travis, you want to go to church?"

"Not really, I just want us to chill around the house, go to the matinee this afternoon, maybe come back home and grill out."

"That's cool. Well, I'm going to get ready for church. It's ten o'clock now. I'm going to leave at eleven. I should be back by two o'clock. We can go after I get back."

I started getting ready for Church. As I ironed my clothes, Travis got up, went into our closet and pulled out a suit.

"What are you doing, Boo?"

"I'm going to church with you."

Church had become a soothing antidote for many of Travis's stresses. My faith in God kept me in this marriage during the rough times. Church had become an important part of our marriage. Worshipping together made our marriage stronger. God became our counselor.

Chapter XII

Surprise

A few months later, Travis and I had planned a huge surprise birthday party for my mom. Travis thought that it was a good idea. I first called my mom's buddies, Roomy, Katie, Montice, Bretta, Brenda, and Ruth to see what they thought. They were really excited about the idea. So we started planning the surprise party at her house in Fort Lauderdale while we were in Georgia. After calling all of her other close friends and our family members, I was informed that they would take care of calling the rest of the gang. I even called her girlfriends in New York and Georgia. They said they wouldn't miss it for the world. We started planning and preparing for the party.

Travis ordered the liquor from Captain's liquors. Spending Friday nights at Captain's became a tradition for Travis and me. Many police, on and off-duty, would start arriving at Captain's around 10:00 p.m., an hour before closing, and stay until 4:00 a.m. talking about current events, politics, and things that happened on their beats. We'd buy our drinks at a discount, sit back, drink, and enjoy the debates and controversy surrounding current events. I got to hear many stories besides the ones Travis told me. I would hear many officers' sides, perspectives, and testimonies that were considered news-breaking incidents for our local television stations' news coverage. At times, there would be at least thirty officers in the store... some accompanied by their spouses or lovers. *This was an interesting experience that was unsurpassable.*

I called Florida to order things such as the cake, champagne fountain, chafing dishes, etc. It didn't make sense to take those items to another state with me, when I could rent them there. We made party favors and musical tapes with mostly oldies, goodies and jazz selections. It was exciting getting ready for the party. Bretta said she would make her famous wings. Roomy helped me do most of the legwork. Katie gathered up more and more people such as Jackie, a new good friend of my mom's, and many others. Now my problem would be getting her out of the house. Well, I left this up to Breezy, one of her boys. A man of intelligence, he was a smooth, suave sailor back in his day. He moved to Daytona Beach from Miami a few years ago to retire from his profession as a CPA. I called him up one night and told him of my plans.

"...Sure thing, Candi, I can handle that. I'll just tell Julia that I'm coming to town and that I want to take her to dinner for her birthday."

"Oh, Breezy, thanks so much. She's going to be ecstatic. I want this party to be very special."

"What time do you want me to pick her up and bring her home?"

"Pick her up at seven and bring her home about nine o'clock. I'll make sure everyone is at the house by nine."

I felt two hours was enough time to get her house ready for the party as long as the food was already cooked.

"No problem, Candi."

We verified the date with each other and then hung up. I decided that the color scheme would be red and gold. Red was her favorite color. It was her sorority's color, also. I chose gold, because it looks elegant with red. These were the colors of her balloons, cake, and party favors. Roomy, Travis and I decided that the menu would consist of wings, meatballs with mushroom sauce, rice, stuffed crabs, boiled shrimp, a vegetable tray, crab salad, potato salad, cake, and plenty of alcohol.

After all of the plans were made, I figured that it would not be hard to surprise her. I knew where she kept her spare key. I also knew that Breezy was very reliable and would follow our plan. So I had enough time to get the house prepared as long as I had everything in place.

Three weeks passed by quickly. Travis and I left for Florida on a Friday. My mom's party was planned for the following night, Saturday. I started getting really nervous as soon as we got to Florida. We stayed with Travis's parents that night. All I thought about, focused on, and talked about, was the party. The next morning, I started running errands. We got the food that I was going to prepare, picked up the cake, and got the chafing dishes as well as the champagne fountain. We ran errands for about four hours. We stopped by my cousin's house to pick up money she gave to contribute financially to the festivities. About four o'clock, we got back to Travis's parents' house. I started making the rice and preparing the meatballs while Travis lay down to watch television. I made sure that all of the items going to my mom's party were packed in the car, such as the cake, party favors, balloons, liquor, etc. After I finished preparing the food, Travis and I went over to Roomy's house. Roomy stayed around the corner from my mom's place. On the way to Roomy's house, Travis started developing a negative attitude.

He blurted out, "You have been such a bitch since we have been here. It's all about your momma's damn birthday party."

Where was this coming from? What was his problem? Hell, I thought we were getting along.

"What are you talking about, Travis?"

"You have totally ignored me and you are acting selfish."

Oh, no, I was not going to let him get me mad that day. I had too much to do to let this distract me.

"Travis, I have been kissing you and paying attention to you. I don't understand. Hell, if anything, today you've been the one acting like dirt. You've dragged around all day when you know we had a lot to do."

"Candi that's not true, you are just an inconsiderate asshole."

"Well, you are a non-understanding motherfucker. And I can't believe you just called me an asshole. I told you I don't appreciate that. I thought we were over the name-calling. Look, I'm not going to even argue with you any more."

"You don't give a shit about me," he said.

"Yes, I do, but I still can't believe you called me an asshole."

The audacity of me to say that after I called him a motherfucker. I was just as wrong as he was. We pulled up to Roomy's house steaming mad at each other. We both got out of the car. He left me behind and rang the doorbell. I got to the door just as Roomy answered it.

"Hey, Roomy," I said.

"Hey, guys. Ya'll come in. Your mother is going to be so surprised." Just then I saw Sandy, my mom's girlfriend from New York. I was so surprised

"Sandy," I yelled, "How are you? I'm so glad to see you."

"Girl, we are going to PAAR-TYY," she said. Roomy had picked her up from the airport that morning.

"Girl, you know I am glad to see you, too. You know what I was thinking? We should all stand outside on the lawn and say *surprise* as your mom and Breezy pull up."

"That sounds like a good idea, Sandy."

Hell, at this point I didn't know what was good and what wasn't. I was too busy trying to keep myself calm, hoping that everything would go smoothly.

I turned to Roomy and said, "Well, Breezy should be over there, by now. Roomy, call over there to see if he is." Travis and I looked at one another and rolled our eyes in disgust. I did have to admit that we had progressed a lot from the days of letting every one know that we were mad at each other. Roomy called my mom. Of course, my mother didn't know I was in town at this point.

"Hey, Julia, how are you doing, girl? Did Breezy come and pick you up for dinner yet?"

She waited for a minute to hear what my mother was saying. We were all quiet and waiting for Roomy's response. Then she said, "Well, tell him I said hi and you guys have a good time. Child, call me when you get back." I swear, she and her friend talked as if they were teenagers.

She hung up the phone and said to us, "Yall, they are getting ready to walk out the door right now."

Just then, Roomy grabbed her dishes and started heading for the door. Travis, Sandy and I got up and followed her.

"I hope she left her extra set of keys in that place she normally leaves them. If she doesn't we are in big trouble. I have no way of getting in," I said, panicking.

On the way to my mom's, Travis and I didn't say a word to each other. When we got to my mom's place, she was gone. I got out of the car and headed straight to the secret place where she kept the extra set of keys. They were there. *Yes*! I said to myself. *Now I hope I can remember the house's alarm code*. Travis got out of the car as Roomy and Sandy pulled up. I opened the door and punched the alarm code into the system. It worked! We all went inside. We started working like horses. It took twenty minutes to unload the car. As soon as we finished, everyone started working on something. Warmth filled the house's atmosphere. We added to the warmth, by placing the red and gold balloons all over the house and putting the party favors in different places. The decorations were simply beautiful. We warmed up the stuffed crabs and finished heating the meatballs. We placed the cake in the corner next to the chandelier.

The tree was filled with red bows. The environment was so soothing that Travis and I started talking to each other as if we hadn't argued in months. We both looked at the house and smiled together as we were impressed with how things were turning out. Travis then started on the champagne fountain, preparing punch for those who didn't consume alcoholic beverages unlike the lushes we were and knew. I started getting dressed after I placed the food in the chafing dishes at the end of my mother's bar. My mother had a bar in the middle of her living room. It was a cute setup. The bar came in handy as she did a lot of entertaining when I was growing up. Before I could finish getting dressed, people started arriving. It was eight-thirty, by then. Sara, Maxine's daughter, and my girl Wendi came in the room to help me get dressed. After getting dressed, I made some last minute preparations such as getting the plates, napkins, and utensils set up.

Wendi and I went over to taste the punch that my sweetheart had made. Wendi took the first sip and said "Oh, Shit! This is terrible. Girl, what happened to this punch?"

I went over to my baby and asked what he'd used. While I asked, he gave me a kiss on the cheek and said, "Baby, this is beautiful. I'm sorry we argued earlier."

I kissed him back and said, "I'm sorry, too. We did a good job! By the way, baby how did you make the punch?"

He said, "Oh, fruit punch, Sprite, and ice."

Damn, he had put ice in it. That's why it was watered down.

I said, "It's not bad, baby. We probably need to add a little more punch and Sprite, that's all. Also, thanks for making this a success."

By, now, people were coming in like flies. There were at least sixty to seventy people there at this time. I asked another one of my mom's boys, Fletcher, to get more punch for us. Boy, my mom sure had a lot of male friends. Though she accumulated several girlfriends over the years, it didn't come close to the number of males she befriended. I guess she and I were a lot alike in that way. It was eight forty-five that evening. Someone told me to pick up the phone.

I didn't hear it ring, but I answered it, "Hello."

"Yeah, Candi, this is Breezy. We are at the restaurant getting ready to head that way. Are you ready for us?"

"Yes, Breezy! Oh, yes! It seems like everyone is here. There are at least seventy people here."

He then said, "Okay, we are on our way." The music was loud, but so good. I could barely hear Breezy. Roomy had gotten one of her DJ friends to provide the music for the party.

"I'm sorry, Breezy, I didn't hear you."

"I said we are coming now. I will be there in fifteen minutes."

"Okay, see you then." I told Travis what Breezy had said. About five minutes later, we told everyone that my mom should be here by nine o'clock. By listening to that Sandy, I made a fool out of myself for a minute. I started telling everyone that we were going to go outside on the lawn and surprise her. Eventually, Roomy and my cousin said, girl that is tacky. Well, hell, I was confused by not thinking clearly due to the excitement by now, so that was my excuse.

It was nine o'clock when I turned off the lights. I soon saw car lights flickering through the blinds. Travis and I were the closest ones to the front door. He was just as excited as I was. He was even closer to the door than I was, moving nervously.

After peeping through the blinds to confirm their arrival, I said loudly, "Everybody, she's here." Everyone started saying, "Shush." You could here a pin drop. Just then, the doorknob started moving. We heard her mumbling something, but we couldn't understand it.

She opened up the door and everyone yelled, "SURPRISE!" I'd never seen such a look on her face. Her mouth was wide open. She looked, and said, "I don't believe this. I don't believe this." She then kept her mouth open as if she were in shock. She continued, "Candi, what, I just don't believe this." She looked at Travis and started laughing. She said kidding, "I'm going to get you for this."

Travis started laughing. Everyone thought Travis was a down- to-earth good person, as well as a comedian. She then started going around the room in astonishment. She said everyone's name aloud as she hugged him or her. She saw friends from Miami, Atlanta, even from New York. Our cousins came from Orlando, also. She told everyone that she could not believe that her daughter and son-in-law pulled this off from another state. I told her that with the help of her dear friends and our relatives, we made it possible. Travis was a better host than I. Travis and I had a wonderful time. He acted more like her offspring than I did. He couldn't believe how nice it had turned out, either. Until four o'clock that morning we ate, partied, and danced to everything from Marvin Gaye and Al Green to Barry White and Chaka Khan. It was a night to remember. After it was over I felt bad about one thing…I had forgotten about my aunt Betty in New Jersey. I had so much on my mind that I forgot. I hope she forgave me for not inviting her.

Travis and I started seeing progress in our relationship by how well we resolved conflicts. Our ability to efficiently resolve conflicts had drastically improved. Differences of opinion were now respected. We learned to give each other space if needed. We even got past the verbal abuse such as nasty name-calling. This was a milestone for us and we were understandably happy about this.

Chapter XIII

The Funeral

The year was 1995. We were tired of living in an apartment. I also became interested in business and investments, because I knew I didn't want to work for anyone else, when I could work for myself. So, I discussed small business and investment ideas over with Travis. Eventually, I was able to convince him to a point where that's all he talked about. We were on the right track. We just really didn't know what type of business we wanted to get involved with. Our first objective was to buy a house.

Travis worked EJ's whenever and wherever he could to pay some bills off as well as decrease our debt. I started working two jobs, a full-time and one part-time, to help accomplish this, also. His EJ's were three to six hours a day, three or four days a week. My second job was twenty hours a week. Soon, I started getting tired and stressed from the demanding schedule that I had. Travis would tell me to quit, but I wanted to help as much as possible. I didn't think it was fair that only he work two jobs in our relationship. We went into this marriage fifty-fifty. Besides, he knew as well as I, that I needed to work a second job to get quicker results.

The tables started turning. I was becoming the catalyst of our problems. After the D.C. and Thanksgiving incident, Travis became a rather calm individual. We started going to counseling to solve his interpersonal conflicts as well as improve the way we resolved conflicts in our marriage.

One day we got a call from my Aunt Beth in Houston. I spent a lot of time with her during my summer vacations when I was a little girl. We had so much fun together. She was an adventurous person. We'd go camping, hiking, fishing, crabbing, etc. We drove to different places including Canada and Mexico. I will never forget the day we saw a dog roasting in the window of a little shack on the border of Mexico. I was shocked, but she told me that poor people lived in this area and that dog is a cuisine for them. I always knew that whenever I was going to spend time with her, we'd always see things that I'd never seen before. Even after she married her husband, Brother Johnson, the excitement escalated. She eventually adopted her nephew, Dent. It then became the four of us during my vacation months. We'd even get with my uncle Dennis, her brother, sometimes. Brother Johnson, a deacon, was just like a blood uncle to me. He was really good to me during my visits. Years later, after I graduated from high school, she adopted Dent's brother and sister, Halley and Bent. Their mother, my other aunt, was diagnosed as schizophrenic.

"Hello, Candi."

"Hey, Auntie Beth."

"Well, honey." She paused then said, "Brother Johnson passed away last night."

"Oh, Beth, I'm so sorry." I really didn't know what to say. Brother Johnson had been sick for a few years. He became dependent on her and her family. He was like an infant. He couldn't do anything for himself. She even had a portion of her house remodeled with handicap access to aid them. So, she expected his death soon.

"Well, Beth, when is the funeral?"

"Next Saturday."

"Travis and I will be there. Beth, again I'm sorry. Brother Johnson was just like a blood relative to me. Do you need anything? Or do you want me to do anything?"

"No, Candi, just be there."

"Okay, I love you."

"I love you, too."

I told Travis about this and he said that it would be cheaper to drive there. Plus, we were trying to get money together for the house. We really couldn't afford to fly. A week passed. It was a Thursday night. Travis had my bags packed for me. He packed my bags when we went away on trips a majority of the times. He was good about things like that.

I had gotten home from working both jobs and was exhausted. Travis took time off work the following two nights. I, only, was off on Friday from my two jobs, as I had the weekends off.

I was very sad about Brother Johnson, but then again, he'd suffered for a long time. It was good that he was not suffering any longer. We got up and left as planned. Travis and I had a very pleasant trip there, but I was drained because I hadn't gotten any sleep the night before. I was also overworked at this time. I was looking forward to seeing many of the uncles that I hadn't seen since I was seven years old. My mom, Maxine, Uncle Deangelo and his wife, Aunt Lillian, were going to be there, also.

When we got to my aunt's house, Maxine and a few other people were there. So they gave us directions to the church at which the wake was to be held. Travis and I washed up and changed into some dressier clothes. Everyone was already at the wake, including my mom, Beth, and many others. As we went inside the church, I felt total sadness when thinking how wonderful Brother Johnson was. Looking at his body was confirmation of the death that I could not bring myself to believe. I then looked over at Dent, whom I hadn't seen in ten years. He was six feet two and as handsome as he could be. He was just ten years old the last time that I had seen him, as tall as my shoulders back then.

After the wake, I went to help my mom comfort Beth. Travis was behind me making sure that I was comforted. After the wake that night, we all went back to Beth's house. I went into one of the bedrooms to change into something more comfortable. I then came out into the living room area and walked up to Travis. There was a table full of food that many people had brought over for family and friends to consume while in mourning. We both stated that we were hungry and proceeded to the table. Before we got to the table, we walked by two women. Both weighed approximately one hundred eighty pounds. Neither one of the women was over five feet, six inches in height.

As I walked by these women, one of them mumbled, "Who does she think she is? Ha, she ain't all that," with a laugh.

Now, why was I the subject of their conversation? Stressed out, tired, and sad I was simply minding my own business. I wasn't interested in being bothered, nor was I interested in bothering anyone. Now, I don't mind saying what I feel, because holding things in irritates and stresses me out. Even so, I didn't respond to the woman's remarks. Travis and I went to the food table. We got our plates and started fixing them. Soon, the same lady who made that comment went to the other side of the table to fix her plate. We both looked at each other, at the same time. She looked at me in an unfriendly odd gesture.

I then said, "Do you have a problem with me?" with a slight attitude.

She said with a nasty tone, "You don't want to go there with me."

"Oh, I'll go there with you." Hell, I hadn't done anything to her. Just then, Travis grabbed me and said, "Candi, leave it alone."

I turned to Travis and said, "Travis, I didn't do anything to this chick."

I guess I shouldn't have kept it going. Today, I wish I wouldn't have, but you live and learn, as my mother always says. She never said anything to me afterward. About thirty seconds later, I heard this loud voice say, "Who are you?"

I looked up and saw this older lady who was in her fifties standing opposite me at the table. I said with an attitude, "I am Candi. I am Beth's niece. And who are you?"

"I'm Leon's sister and her mother." She pointed to the chick I had the confrontation with. Leon was Brother Johnson's first name.

She repeated herself, "I said who are you?" Her tone was loud and extremely ignorant. Hell, was she drunk?

I'd already told her who I was. "I said, I was Beth's niece." I was really frustrated at this point. Her daughter and I were finished with our little conflict. Nonetheless, this lady was instigating another confrontation. Travis was still holding me. The lady and I both moved away from the table and in front of each other. I wasn't thinking that we would fight. That's not my style. I just wanted be firm in what I was saying and stand up for myself.

Just then, my uncle Dennis got between us and said, "What's going on?" He was obviously concern with our inappropriate behavior. He looked at the lady as he spoke, maybe because he'd thought she was an older and wiser person. He wasn't trying to escalate the problem, only solve it. Before I could say anything, everyone started coming over to see what was going on. There were at least fifty people in the house, including the preacher, a few deacons, several of Leon's family members, and many of mine. Someone from Brother Johnson's side of the family rushed over thinking that Uncle Dennis was taking my side. I was bewildered at how this situation had gotten out of hand so rapidly.

This guy approached Uncle Dennis as if he were ready to fight. What kinds of people are in this family? At this time, Travis was in shock. Can you believe that Mr. "I will beat anybody down, if they step on my shoes" was in shock? Hell, now I guess he knew how I felt when he placed me in appalling situations like this. Uncle Dennis saw this guy's expression and action. He then positioned himself as if he were ready to fight. Just then, several people grabbed them both. The house was noisy and full of chaos. My mother and Aunt Lillian came over to me and took me from Travis. We then went outside. As soon as we got outside, my aunt started rubbing my back and comforting me. My mother couldn't believe what had just happened. She was shocked, but not as much as Travis was. You could hear all of the noise inside. I think both families were inside arguing. At this time, I was calm, but totally EMBARRASSED unable to blame anyone but myself. Several of my family members were highly religious people. I didn't want to be viewed by them as a loud, ignorant troublemaker. Also, I didn't want to embarrass my mom. Soon I heard a voice that sounded loud enough to hear one-half a mile away. It was powerful and very clear from where I was standing near the street. The windows and doors of the house were even closed.

"WAIT A MINUTE...JUST WAIT A GODDAMN MINUTE. EVERYBODY NEEDS TO SHUT THE HELL UP OR GET THE HELL OUT." It was the voice of the deacon. Everyone got quiet!

Soon, that loud-mouthed woman came outside. She was still talking shit. I could not cuss her out the way I wanted to, as my aunt and mom were standing there. She went over to her car, which was opposite from where we were standing. Someone was over there telling her to get in the car and go home.

She then said, "I can't believe you guys are taking that pipsqueak's side."

No, she didn't call me a pipsqueak. I didn't say anything, because I would have looked as stupid as she did. Plus, I couldn't do that in front of my relatives. I had already looked like shit. I had too much respect for them. Soon, the loud mouth woman left. Travis was still in shock. He and my mother ran to the store to get some liquor. He even told me that this situation scared him. What! I found that hard to believe. I started thinking about Beth. Then, I really felt bad. She had gone to her room during the incident. I felt as if I had let her down, being a part of that situation. I know she was disappointed in me. She and my mother told me that things happen and people's emotions are the greatest at weddings and funerals.

The following day, the limousines came to Beth's house. I didn't even want to go to the funeral. I didn't want to show my face. I wish I could have just shrunk until I disappeared that weekend. Nonetheless, Travis was shoulder to shoulder with me. He didn't seem to be embarrassed though he was probably more embarrassed than I. Everyone was at the house about ten o'clock that morning. I saw the loud-mouthed woman and her daughter. They acted as if nothing had happened the night before. We were all going to leave from there. Only the immediate and close family members were riding in the limousine. Beth told us that we were on the list to ride in the limousine. We all went outside for our seating assignments. Travis and I looked and laughed when we saw who was giving out the seating arrangements.

Travis said, "Candi, look who's giving out the seating assignments."

I said with a smirk, "Oh, shit. The girl I had the problem with."

"Hell, we'll probably end up in the trunk, if it is her decision," Travis said.

"Boy, you are crazy," I said.

She was unexpectedly cordial with us when she told us which limousine we were riding in. After the immediate family got into the limousines and everyone else in cars, we left for the funeral. On the way to the funeral, Travis had me laughing so hard. I guess that was his way of easing the pain I was feeling at the time due to the death of Brother Johnson as well as the incident that occurred the night before.

"Candi," Travis started setting up a joke. I could tell by the tone of his voice. "We're all going to get to the funeral. You and that girl are going to start fighting. Then you guys will start throwing flowers and Bibles everywhere. One of the flowers is going to hit the casket. Then Brother Johnson is going to jump out of the casket and say, 'Now hold on, wait a minute.'" Travis was a fool. I know a lot of people may not see the humor in that, but that was his way of making me laugh. Travis had a tendency to paint humorous pictures from bitter, nasty, perplexing scenes to help the sufferer feel some comfort.

That's why people loved him. Everyone knew he was a funny, lovable, and enjoyable individual. I thought this, but not all the time. They didn't have to live with him and see his dark side. But nobody is perfect, right? Besides, I had a dark side as well. STAY TUNED….

Chapter XIV

Locked Up

It was three months after the funeral incident. The year was 1996. I was still working a second job. Travis was working more extra jobs than ever. His patrol hours had changed from 11:00 p.m.-7:00 a.m. to 3:00 p.m.-11:00 p.m. This was okay with me. By the time I finished with my two jobs, came home, and got it together, he was walking in the door. It worked out for him, also, because most of the good EJ's were in the morning. We weren't hurting financially, but we were physically. I was hurting mentally, also.

Overworked and stressed, I wasn't getting enough sleep. Travis seemed as though he had it all under control. He was dealing with stress from the job better now, while I started losing my mind.

Because we had counseling sessions after the D.C. incident, Travis' ability to resolve conflicts efficiently at home as well as at work improved. We also focused on our roles and responsibilities for strengthening our marriage. We never talked about my problems or temperament, though.

I was also under a lot of pressure, because we had started a security patrol business. We had one client. One client wasn't much, but at this time it was worth a fortune to us. You have to start somewhere…and we had at least gotten started! Though Travis had the expertise in the field, I handled most of business operations, as he couldn't leave his patrol duty whenever he wanted unless it was life/death circumstances. I had more flexibility in leaving my job than he, if something happened. During this time all the weight of our business fell on me. Our employee's hours were scheduled roughly the same time that Travis patrolled the streets. I took care of our business's time sheets, payroll, and ensured customer satisfaction. It was too much for me to handle, but I held the fort down. Travis picked up the slack every now and then, but he didn't have the time, flexibility, and availability, to allow him to contribute, frequently.

Fortunately, despite our hectic routine, our relationship was starting to become beautiful. Travis knew how much I loved Lexus automobiles. I talked about them every time I saw one. I told him how I couldn't wait to have one. I talked about this more than I did about buying a house. Wasn't that a shame? Well, maybe; then, maybe not. It's where you put your priorities. You have to live your life. If your priorities are all screwed up, then you will suffer the consequences of bad decision-making. Hell, if someone wants a smooth ride, but has nowhere to sleep or park it, then that's their business.

One day, I pulled up to the apartment building. I was so tired. Travis saw me pulling up, waited till I got to our front door, opened it and handed me a key with a slanted gold "L" inscribed. I yelled at the top of my lungs, "I love you." I went outside, looked at the car, ran back upstairs, jumped up and down over him. Later that evening, we signed the contract to own the vehicle. I think he felt bad about the long hours I worked. *What the Hell! I'm going to buy my wife and myself a Lexus. I feel we deserve it*, he figured.

My mother told me a while back that she would be coming to see me for about four days. She was scheduled to come in on Wednesday of the last week in July. I looked forward to this, as she hadn't visited with me for several years. I decided to take off work the day that she came as well as the rest of the week. I was really excited. I planned a full day for us on every day that she would be here.

It was soon Wednesday morning. Her plane was scheduled to come in at ten o'clock that morning. I picked her up and took her to my place. She unpacked her bags and talked to Travis for an hour or so. We then went to the Cheesecake Factory for lunch. Afterward, we headed for the outlet malls in Forsyth County. After browsing in the stores, it was about six o'clock, so we went home, relaxed, and ate pizza. Travis came home with her favorite bottle of liquor, Dewar's.

The following day, I took her to my workplace. I'd scheduled her for a human factors study on a new product our company had just designed. For two and a half hours of her time, the company gave her and each member of her study group lunch and fifty dollars. She enjoyed it. Afterward, we went to another outlet mall and stayed there for a few hours. It was six o'clock by then. It was time for us to go home and get ready to attend the dinner theater that I'd purchased tickets for in advance. The *Phantom of the Opera* started at eight o'clock that evening and it lasted until eleven-thirty. The food and entertainment were superb.

The next day, Friday, I fixed breakfast for her, Travis, and three of my cousins that resided in Georgia. They were my cousin Annabelle's kids. We had turkey sausage; potatoes and onions; eggs; and hot, soft, cinnamon rolls. Umm, Umm, Umm! Afterward, we ended up at the CNN center for "Talk-back Live." My mom took a picture with Susan, the host of the talk show. We then took a CNN tour. Following our CNN tour, we went to a seafood restaurant and stuffed ourselves. That night I was drained. Mom's flight was scheduled for seven o'clock the following morning. We didn't go to bed until twelve-thirty. She, Travis and I stayed up talking.

The next morning, I got up at six-thirty, so that I could drop her off at the airport. We were running late, so we started rushing. We looked outside and noticed that it was raining hard. This would require more time in getting to the airport. I lived only seven minutes from the airport, but she still had to check her bags in. So we didn't waste a moment that morning. Because we were rushing out the door, I hadn't notice that I'd forgot my wallet. My driver's license and car insurance papers were inside it.

We'd just arrived at the airport. My car was still running, but parked in the second lane from the terminal and baggage check-in. My mom and I both got out of the car. I started helping her with her luggage. The baggage guy grabbed the bags from both of us and set them in the baggage check-in area. I gave her a hug and a kiss. I watched her go to the baggage check-in area. I headed to the driver's side of my car. I didn't get in the car, totally. I put my right leg inside of the car and I leaned on the left leg. I could see that my mom was just getting ready to leave the baggage area and head for her flight's gate. As I was starting to sit in the car, this young lady dressed in a uniform came up to the car. She wasn't a police officer, but a "ticket writer" for the airport. The airport was in the jurisdiction of the department my husband worked for.

She said, "You need to move your car. NOW!"

Well, that's what I was getting ready to do. But, why was she talking to me like that? I could understand this tone, if she had been repeating herself. I guess if you are hired in a position of authority, you can talk to the public however you want. However, this was a tense period in my life and I wasn't in a good mood.

"You don't ask me like that. I move when I want to," I said. Now, I knew I was wrong, but I really didn't care. I was tired, overworked, and stressed. I really didn't give a shit about the consequences. I wasn't going to take it from her or anyone else that day.

"Well, I'll just write you out a ticket," she said

"Honey, you can do whatever you want. I'll just give the ticket to my husband, because he's a cop. He'll take care of it for me. So do what you want to do."

In the past, I'd gotten out of several speeding tickets because the officer presiding said it was a common courtesy to let the family members of officers off the hook as long as they weren't abusing the law. Immediately she left. I sat in the car. I then put my foot on the brake and placed the car in drive. As I was ready to drive off, I noticed her and a police officer approaching my car. He worked for the same department as Travis. He just wasn't in the same precinct.

He yelled at the top of his voice, "MOVE YOUR DAMN CAR."

Oh, wait a minute. Just wait a damn minute; like that deacon said the night of Brother Johnson's wake. I knew how Travis had gotten complaints from citizens who said that he was unnecessarily rude. Officers could, eventually, get suspended, if they received too many reported complaints. Some complaints were illegitimate; for instance family members who witnessed the arrests of their loved ones would get offended and fabricate complaints on the arresting officers for the purposes of retaliation. In other cases, the complaints were justifiable. Okay, so this guy was wrong for screaming at me, but I was wrong for not moving the car immediately. Everyone seemed to have had a stick up the ass that day.

"Don't you talk to me like that," I said. "I was going to move, but I don't appreciate the tone of your voice or hers. I was just getting ready to pull off, when she started this."

Not paying any attention to the words that I'd just uttered, he continued to yell.

"I SAID, MOVE THIS CAR."

The lady then said to him, "Yeah, she said she didn't care if we gave her a ticket because her husband is a police officer and he'll take care of it."

"Oh, really." He started nodding his head, and he said, "Okay," then started walking away. I wasn't waiting for shit. I was steaming by now. So, I drove off. Hell, this is what I was trying to do, before that "ticket-writing" chick approached me.

I hadn't driven fifty feet before I looked in my rear view mirror and saw the police officer in his patrol car with sirens screaming and lights flashing. *Okay*, I said to myself, *this motherfucker wants me to stop now, but he wanted me to move a few seconds ago*. At this time, I was almost at the end of the terminal. I couldn't pull over in either direction, because cars were driving on each side of me. So I drove a few more feet to the end of the terminal. I was getting ready to pull over in the lane closest to the terminal when he moved his car diagonally in front of my car. He blocked me off…yeah, like I was really trying to elude him. I should have taken the names of these "law enforcement" personnel and left. Unfortunately, I escalated the problem by speaking what I felt. God forbid if you respectfully tell some police officers what's on your mind. All hell will break loose. After pulling beside and slightly in front of me, he got out of his car and came up to mine.

"Get out of the car, please." He wasn't as rude as he had been, initially. He knew that he was going to stick it to me. That's why.

I got out of the car and said, “You better not put a single fuckin’ hand on me. I mean it.”

What was I thinking? I was totally out of my mind for saying this. I guess Travis and I had switched roles. I got out of my car and the officer opened his back car door. He didn’t touch me at all. Maybe he didn’t due to the potential implications and major conflicts that could occur if he were aggressive as he knew I was a police officer’s wife.

“Get in the car, ” he ordered me and stepped away from the back door, so that I could sit down. I got in the car. He closed the door.

“Call your damn supervisor, right now,” I said. “I was getting ready to move, but you had no right to talk to me the way you did.”

“I need your driver’s license and insurance card, ma’am.”

“Don’t have it.” *Shit*, I said to myself. That’s right, I was in so much of a rush that I had forgotten them both. I wasn’t nervous yet. I was just pissed off.

“Ma’am, what’s your name?”

“You need to be concerned about Travis Dixon, my husband.” I don’t think he heard the “my husband” part, because he thought I said Travis Dixon.

He got on the radio and called his supervisor. He started writing out ticket after ticket after ticket. He wrote about six tickets in the name of Travis Dixon.

“What in the hell are you writing out all those tickets for?” I asked angrily.

He said nothing. Soon his supervisor came up to the car. "Yes, ma'am, what's the problem?" his supervisor said.

"I am so damn pissed off at this officer. He is rude as hell. I was getting ready to move my car, but he came up to me and yelled in my ear telling me to move my damn car. He's unfair. I did nothing more than tell him to talk to me in a better tone."

"Well, ma'am, that's too bad. He told you to move, but you didn't." Then he stepped away from the car and left. The officer who pulled me over picked up the radio and said, "I'm getting ready to take her down now."

I thought to myself, what in the world did he mean by *down*? Oh, I guess I was under arrest. He never told me that I was under arrest. Shit, there are people whose loved ones' death was caused by assailants still running free, as well as many other unsolved crimes of innocent victims, and he was arresting me 'cause I expressed my dislike for his tone of voice? Something was terribly wrong.

"Oh, so I guess I'm going to jail," I said.

"Yes," he replied.

"Okay, whatever. All you guys can go to hell!"

Just then, the tow truck arrived. They started to impound my car.

"And I better not have one single scratch on my car." Did I know when to shut up? I guess not. I was so irate at this point that I didn't care.

He took me downtown to the city jail. It was about nine o'clock in the morning by then. For some reason, I still wasn't nervous. I still wasn't surprised about the situation I was in, either. On the other hand, I never thought I would ever see the inside of a jail.... not as a prisoner anyway. I was, for the most part, a "goody-two-shoe" as far as the law was concerned. Maybe in the back of my mind I wasn't worried because I knew that Travis worked in this jurisdiction. He would be able take care of this whole thing. The officer opened the car door and told me to get out.

"Yeah, I am, just don't put your hands on me," I said.

He didn't. They opened the door from the inside, once they saw us coming up. When we got inside, a female officer started searching me. After searching me, she took me to a huge holding area. One side of the room had small booths at which detention officers checked the inmates in. Another side of the room contained several rooms enclosed in clear, bulletproof glass windows. The middle of the room had many rows of benches facing different directions. The men sat on one side of the room and the women sat on the other. Pay phones were situated in the middle of the room. One could make as many phone calls as he or she had quarters. People were everywhere. I saw prostitutes and crack-heads. There were a few people in handcuffs, but the majorityof those arrested weren't cuffed. I remembered this lady whose clothes were torn and dirty.

I heard her on the phone. "Mo-maa, please com'git me out a hea. You can git da money, by puttin' the house up. You did it fo' junior, na why you can't do it fo me?"

Then she hung the phone up, and said, "Fuck it." She turned around and looked at me, "What chu in hea fo?"

I said, "Being rude to an officer as he was rude to me."

"How you gone git outta hea?"

"I hope my husband."

Then I thought to myself, *MY HUSBAND*. Ah, ooh, he is going to be pissed. I don't even have any money on me to call him, because I walked out the house empty-handed this morning. I FINALLY GOT NERVOUS.

A detention officer had been trying to flirt with me while I was in there, but I didn't pay him any attention until I found out I had no money, not even a quarter with which to call Travis. So I walked up to the detention officer and asked him, "Hey look, I know you guys don't allow prisoners to use the employee phone, but I don't have any money. My husband works for the city as an officer and I really need to call him. I know he's going to be pissed off when I tell him where I am."

Oh, I was nervous then. Yeah, I should have thought about all that before I had gotten myself in this situation. I did all that preaching to Travis about keeping his temper under control, yet I was in trouble for loosing control, now.

The detention officer looked at me and said, "No, you can't use our phones. You are right. We don't let prisoners use them."

Shit, I didn't want to stay in this motherfucker much longer. What was I going to do? I went and sat back down.

Five minutes later, he came up to me and said, "Follow me." I got up and did just that. He took me to one of the phones used by the detention officers.

"What are you in here for? What could you have possibly done?" asked the detention officer.

"I was rude with a police officer, because he was rude to me."

"And you said your husband is a police officer? Ha ha." He thought that was real funny.

He continued, "You can use this phone. Just dial nine, then the number."

I said, "Thanks so much. I really appreciate this, sir. I really do."

So, I started dialing my home phone number. After dialing, I heard the phone ringing. My heart started beating faster. I didn't know what he'd say. I could barely bring myself to tell him where I was. I surely wasn't going to tell anyone else about this.

"Hello," Travis answered eagerly as if he was hoping it was I.

"Hello, Travis."

"Where are you? It's almost ten o'clock. You left the house around seven to take your mom to the airport. I have been worrying sick about you. I paged you but you left your pager home."

"I'm in ah,...?" I stopped. Then I said to myself, G*irl just say it, hell*. "I'm in jail," I said swiftly.

"Get the fuck out of here, Candi. Now stop playing."

"Travis, I'm serious. I'm downtown on..." After I told him what street I was on and what part of the building they brought me in, he knew I was telling the truth.

"Damn it, Candi!" I'd never heard him as frustrated and disappointed in me as I heard him on this day. He said, "What did you do? I don't believe this. My wife is in jail."

"Well, a police officer got smart with me. So we exchanged a few words and..."

He cut me off. "I told you that you can't go around talking to people any fuckin' way you want."

"Travis, I don't. I just want to stand up for myself."

"All right. Now, I have to go to the bail bondsman for you and... Damn it, Candi. Look I'll be down there as soon as I can. Bye!"

"Okay, bye..." He'd already hung up on me. He was pissed. Well, now I was starting to feel bad. Hell, he knew for a second time how I felt when he took me through a similar situation. I went back over to where I was sitting, then the detention officer walked up to me.

"Well, what did he say?"

"Oh, he was pissed. He's coming to get me, right now."

I continued to look at the others in my presence. I saw this guy who looked like he was straight out of Wall Street. He was a well-dressed, clean-cut individual. I wondered to myself what was he in for. I then saw this twentish guy that looked like he'd been playing in the mud all night. He had traces of blood on his face and arms. The place smelled as if one hundred people had played four hours of full-court basketball a week ago, but hadn't taken a shower since then. This smell was mixed with scents of shit and urine. I was ready to get the hell out of there.

Forty-five minutes after I had gotten off the phone, I saw Travis at the entrance that I came in. I was so glad to see him. He'd gone over to the bail bondsman to post my bail. The bondsman posted my bail without charge, as Travis was an officer. He had his helpful connections. No one other than police officers, detention officers, and prisoners was allowed in the area. Travis showed his badge and came inside the building. Everyone knew he was an officer because he had his gun on the side of his waist. He came over to me and said that he'd talk to someone about rushing my paperwork, so that I could get out quickly. Usually, people stay in jail for a day or two before they go to the next step, which is out on bond or to a private cell. He worked some miracles that day because I was out forty-five minutes after he got there. Well, because he brought criminals to this facility, the detention officers were familiar with him as well as he was with their system. During the forty-five minutes, they took my picture, fingerprinted me, and processed my paperwork.

The girl who was on the phone with her mother earlier, said, "Gull, who dat is?"

By now everyone knew he was an officer and he was there to bail me out.

"My husband," I said.

When they finished the process, it was time for us to go. I had to go out a certain exit. So Travis told me that he'd wait for me outside. There were ten people in this room before the exit door. Everyone in that room was amazed at how fast I had gotten out of there. They had all been in there for at least twenty-four hours or more. Frankly, I wasn't supposed to be there in the first place. Maybe this was a lesson for me that "some things are better left unsaid." Also, that "you can't always out-talk everyone out talk you."

Well, Travis was also very upset with the officer. He ran into him at the impounding division of their department when picking up the car. He and Travis exchanged a few words that weren't so nice. This officer didn't care for Afro-Americans as later one of his coworkers stressed. The officer admitted that he had an attitude with me, but he said that I didn't have to act the way I did. Travis and his friends considered "paying him a little Visit," but decided to let it go.

Travis was silent for the first ten minutes of our car ride home. Then he broke the silence by saying, "Candi, I just need to know…what in the hell got into you?"

"I don't know, Boo."

"I'm so upset with you that I could kill you. I can't believe that my wife has caused me such embarrassment…and in the department that I work for to top it off. I don't want to say anything to you, because I may say the wrong thing and upset you. So, I would appreciate it if you don't say anything to me right now."

"Okay, fine… I won't. I can respect that."

Well, I had not said anything in the first place, because I could feel how upset he was. Nonetheless, he was a statesman about the entire situation. After this encounter, he never said anything else about this incident to me again ever. After going to court several months later, I ended up getting a year's probation and twenty hours of community service.

Chapter XV

Home Sweet Home

In October of 1996, we eagerly anticipated the sweet taste of being homeowners. We were very close to it. We had given the mortgage broker one thousand dollars as our good-faith money. We decided to stay with Derrick months before our closing date. He lived about thirty-five minutes east of Atlanta. He also lived down the street from his mom. Derrick told us to move in with him so that we could make sure that we had enough money at the "closing table." In turn, Travis said that he'd give him money here and there.

A week later, we got out of our apartment lease, packed all of our things and moved in with Derrick. Our mortgage broker told us that everything was looking good and that moving with Derrick would be a good idea to ensure enough money at closing. A lot of our bills were paid off, due to the overtime and EJ's we'd worked. The ones that weren't paid off, we paid in installments. *All of the things that we had gone through created a strong bond between us. We were, basically, inseparable. This is what I said when we met; only this type of inseparability was a healthful one.* We each deeply respected the other. Not only did we have much love, but a lot of respect for one another. Trust was something that we were both finding in each other.

Two weeks after we'd moved into Derrick's house, our mortgage broker and real estate agent left a message on the voice mail at my office, after I'd left work. They said that we weren't going to be able to qualify for a house. After I got home and checked my voice mail, I wondered what we'd do. I immediately told Travis. He was off this day. We called the broker and agent to find out what was going on, but neither one could be reached. We decided that we would figure out what we'd do over dinner. We'd already broken our lease and Derrick's house was just a one-and-a-half-month arrangement.

When we had gotten back from dinner, Derrick's mom had left a note stating that it was time to pay rent of approximately five hundred dollars. We really didn't have that amount of money, as every dime except that going to Derrick was spoken for. Travis and Derrick had already agreed on an arrangement, at least that's what Travis and I thought. I knew that five hundred dollars for rent was not much, but when you have made prior arrangements to pay a little here and there, it was much.

We started worrying about what we'd do. Travis spoke with Derrick and found out that his mom took it upon herself to get involved, when she didn't know what was agreed upon, initially. Travis and I got placed in the middle of Derrick and his mother's altercation. The next day, we called the mortgage broker and real estate agent. They told us that the factual credit report showed them things that we never mentioned in the beginning, which made our debt ratio too high. The difference between a regular credit report and a factual credit report is that the factual report is a collaboration of many credit bureaus, whereas the regular report comes from only one credit bureau. Most of the items that she was referring to had been paid already. We just needed to get letters from the creditor saying so. This was encouraging to us.

Derrick's mom still wanted us to pay five hundred dollars for rent, but Derrick said to pay what was agreed upon. So every day there was a note from his mom telling us that we owed her. This put a strain on Travis and Derrick's relationship. Despite the fact that an agreement wasn't initially made with her, we gave her a few dollars here and there, anyway. We didn't have money to give her, but with God's help we found a way. Travis continued giving Derrick money, also.

A few weeks passed. It was early November in 1997. The ground was covered lightly with snow. The day of on our home closing was here. After the closing at the lawyer's office, we were so happy we didn't know what to do with ourselves. We had finished with all the paperwork, walk-through, and procedures by three o'clock that day. We had both taken off the following workday to move into our new home.

We were moving to suburbs thirty miles away from the environment that Travis worked in daily. It was serene in our neighborhood, free of corner drug pushers, streets covered with nickel bags, crack-heads walking back and forth on the same street with nothing else to do, and the sounds of ambulance and police car sirens piercing your eardrums. This environment helped him to block out all of the things that he witnessed at work daily. He noticed that those who lived in the city might have more problems shutting work off, as they live in the same element that they work in.

We decided to put together a dinner celebration with just the two of us. We packed our things into a U-haul truck two days before closing. We also packed an overnight bag that consisted of our immediate needs, such as toothpaste, soap, towels and two extra outfits each in case we weren't up for unpacking our clothes as well as other items on the first night in our new home. We unloaded the bed, a few blankets, television, and a small hand-held radio from the U-haul into the living room. As we didn't have our kitchenware unloaded we decided on getting food that was already prepared. After unloading those items, we took a shower and put on some fresh clothes.

We headed to a chicken rotisserie restaurant and ordered our food to go. We couldn't be elaborate with our plans because we like many others, had spent all of our earnings and savings on purchasing a new home. As soon as we approached the counter Travis said, "Umm, that spinach casserole looks good."

"It sure does. Let's get that and some rice pilaf," I said.

"Ma'am, I'd like to order a whole rotisserie chicken and two sides, one spinach casserole and the other rice pilaf. Oh, a cheesecake, also."

The cashier said, "For here or to go?"

Travis replied, "To go."

On our way out of the restaurant Travis said, "Where's my kiss?"

I replied, "It'll cost you a lot."

"Well, you better give it to me on credit, 'cause we are scrapin' the bottom of the barrel, there cutie."

We laughed and kissed each other.

"Oh, Travis, I almost forgot. Ask the cashier for some paper plates, forks, and napkins."

"Okay, there cutie."

After he got those items, we walked out with our bags and proceeded to the liquor store. Where else? We bought a bottle of champagne and two wineglasses since the ones we owned were packed away. After we left the liquor store, we made our last stop at a grocery store. We bought a tray of broiled shrimp with cocktail sauce. This was our appetizer. When we got home, we got our various bags of food out of the car, went into the house and proceeded to the kitchen. We took the food out of their bags. I tuned our hand-held radio to a jazz station. He grabbed my hands and started dancing with me for a few minutes. After dancing, I went and got our blanket from the living room and laid it down in the dining room. We placed all of the food in the center of the blanket. I neatly created our place settings and we both sat down. We held hands, said grace, and began fixing our plates. After our plates were fixed, Travis opened up the bottle of wine and poured wine into the glasses.

"Let's make…," we both started the sentence at the same time.

"I'd like to make a toast to my beautiful wife, to our beautiful home, and our beautiful relationship. Candi, you are my love, my life, my everything."

"Awwwee, I'm touched…and to you, my dear I am very happy especially after jumping over all of the hurdles we faced. Sometimes one has to experience the pain before they can appreciate all of the joy to be gained….you are my love, my life, Travis, you are my everything."

As months progressed, Derrick found himself in trouble and it wasn't for selling drugs. He'd been accused of selling stolen car tag stickers. His "best friend" a fellow officer Jacob, got caught with the stolen tags. Jacob got the heat off himself by giving Derrick's name to Internal Affairs. Derrick was innocent of this crime, though. Travis and a few other guys in their clique were questioned as well, but nothing ever came of it. Eventually, Derrick went to jail and got suspended from the force for a year. Several months ago, Derrick was acquitted of the crime. He was taken off of suspension and was asked to come back to the police department. He didn't want his job back, but in order to get his back-pay salary owed by the city, he had to go back.

Also during this period, I achieved closure in a part of my life. My father was trying to be an integral part of my life now. He started calling me at work a couple of times a week. He told me that people do things for a reason, but sometimes they aren't always right in doing what they do. In the past, he was bitter about his and my mom's divorce. So, he decided to take it out on her by turning his back on me. Well, she was not the one who was fatherless. He admitted his faults and regrets of not spending time with me in the past. He told me it was really painful to think of all the years that slipped away, in which we didn't get a chance to spend time together. At first, I didn't want him back in my life because my mother was my father and mother, but I realized that I would carry the burden of guilt later in life of never accepting him. I didn't want God to punish me for being unforgiving, so I accepted him in my life. We have a beautiful relationship today.

Epilogue

My husband and I are Candi and Travis, in most respects. We experienced a lot of hard knocks through our ten years of marriage. Most of the problems we experienced were during his rookie years. Although we had problems before his "tour of duty" as an officer, a majority of the tragedies and misfortunes of the relationship developed as a result of his career. I do admit that several things we went through challenged the longevity of our relationship, but anything worth having is worth working for. Maybe the extremities of our problems are indicative of the older generation's meaning of tough times. The older generation says, "In today's generation, couples just don't stick it out during the 'tough times' the way we did in ours."

Though a lot of stress and problems through my husband's "rookie years" trickled down to the marriage, I have not been innocent of contributing to the problems. We both did. From my bitching, his stress rages and our thoughts and desires of infidelity, we seemed doomed to fail. Neither one of us was ready for marriage. If we were emotionally ready, would we have still gone through those things? We were immature, silly, and disrespectful toward each other as well as to ourselves. *Remember, you must love and deeply respect yourself, before you can do the same for others.*

Despite our individual and interpersonal tragedies, our love for each other outweighed everything. Though we don't claim to be the most religious people in the world, we have always kept God in our lives. We got on our knees and prayed together time and time again. God and a lot of unconditional love were the underlying factors that kept and continue to keep our marriage glued together. *Today, we serve God together. This has made our spirituality and marriage stronger than ever.* Through our marriage, I realized that anything is possible in life. Today, we are a successful couple and happy with our relationship. Finally, though we are not immune to occasional marital problems, we are respectful, loving, considerate, and patient with each other when solving them. People can change, but, remember, they have to be willing. You can't make them.

Afterword

Married to the Badge was written to assure those who may be going through similar challenging situations that through faith, determination, love and faith in God, anything is possible. As all of my characters in this book are fictional, I as well as many others have experienced similar issues, situations, problems, and the triumphs of a marriage despite the professions of the two people. While problems faced by many couples are equal to or greater than what these characters faced, some marriages don't involve any of these problems. Nonetheless, by working through your problems like Candi and Travis (or my husband and I), your marriage or relationship can produce an unlimited amount of joy and happiness, if you and your mate put your hearts, minds, and souls into it.

Conclusions

I conclude this book with the following *TIPS FOR A HEALTHY RELATIONSHIP:*

A. LOVE YOURSELF. ***You can't love someone else without loving yourself first. Loving yourself allows you to only accept from others the level of respect that you give to yourself.***
B. SHOWER YOUR MATE WITH LOVE. ***Everyone loves to be loved.***
C. ENSURE YOUR MATE HAS ENOUGH SPACE. ***Smothering your mate is a sure way of driving him/her away.***
D. COMPLIMENT YOUR SPOUSE OR MATE.
E. CREATE A ROMANTIC HAVEN SO THAT YOU CAN FULFILL EACH OTHER'S FANTASIES.
F. WHATEVER IT TOOK TO GET YOUR MATE...CONTINUE TO DO.
G. COMMUNICATE. ***It may take a minute up to several hours to get your point across. So take a break, if you have to. Communicate to find cooperative results and to express your desires. It works!***
H. SEEK SPIRITUAL GUIDANCE.
I. KNOW WHEN TO SEEK COUNSELING AFTER ALL YOUR OPTIONS ARE EXHAUSTED.
J. KNOW THAT THE GRASS IS RARELY GREENER. W***hoever you get with, problems are inevitable. If you have someone who loves you and sincerely tries to work through your problems, stick it out with him or her.***
K. KNOW WHEN TO "BACK OFF." ***Know when to back down.***

About the Author

Kimberly Carol Williams Davis and her husband live in Atlanta where she is writer and computer support employee for a State University. She holds an MCSE and a two-year degree in electrical engineering. She currently attends Georgia State University where she is working on a degree in psychology which she plans to use to counsel couples whose marriages are in trouble.

For my Readers

Dear Reader,

Thank you for purchasing Married to the Badge. A portion of the proceeds will be donated to benefit the ***American Heart Association***, the ***Metro Atlanta Police Emerald Society***, and the ***Association for Abused Women & Children***. If you have any questions or comments, feel free to send them to the following address:

Kimberly Davis

P.O. Box 2311

Atlanta, Georgia 30303-2311

E-mail Gafill817@aol.com

I hope this easy reader has been exciting, yet entertaining for you.

May God Bless You,

Kimberly Carol Williams Davis